John Come Down the Backstay

John Come Down the Backstay

Caroline Tapley

Illustrated by Richard Cuffari

Atheneum 1974 New York

This is, in its essentials, a true story.

Library of Congress catalog card number 73-84839
ISBN 0-689-30149-9
Published simultaneously in Canada by
McClelland & Stewart, Ltd.
Manufactured in the United States of America
by Quinn & Boden Company, Inc.
Rahway, New Jersey
Designed by Nancy Gruber
First Edition

For Beth

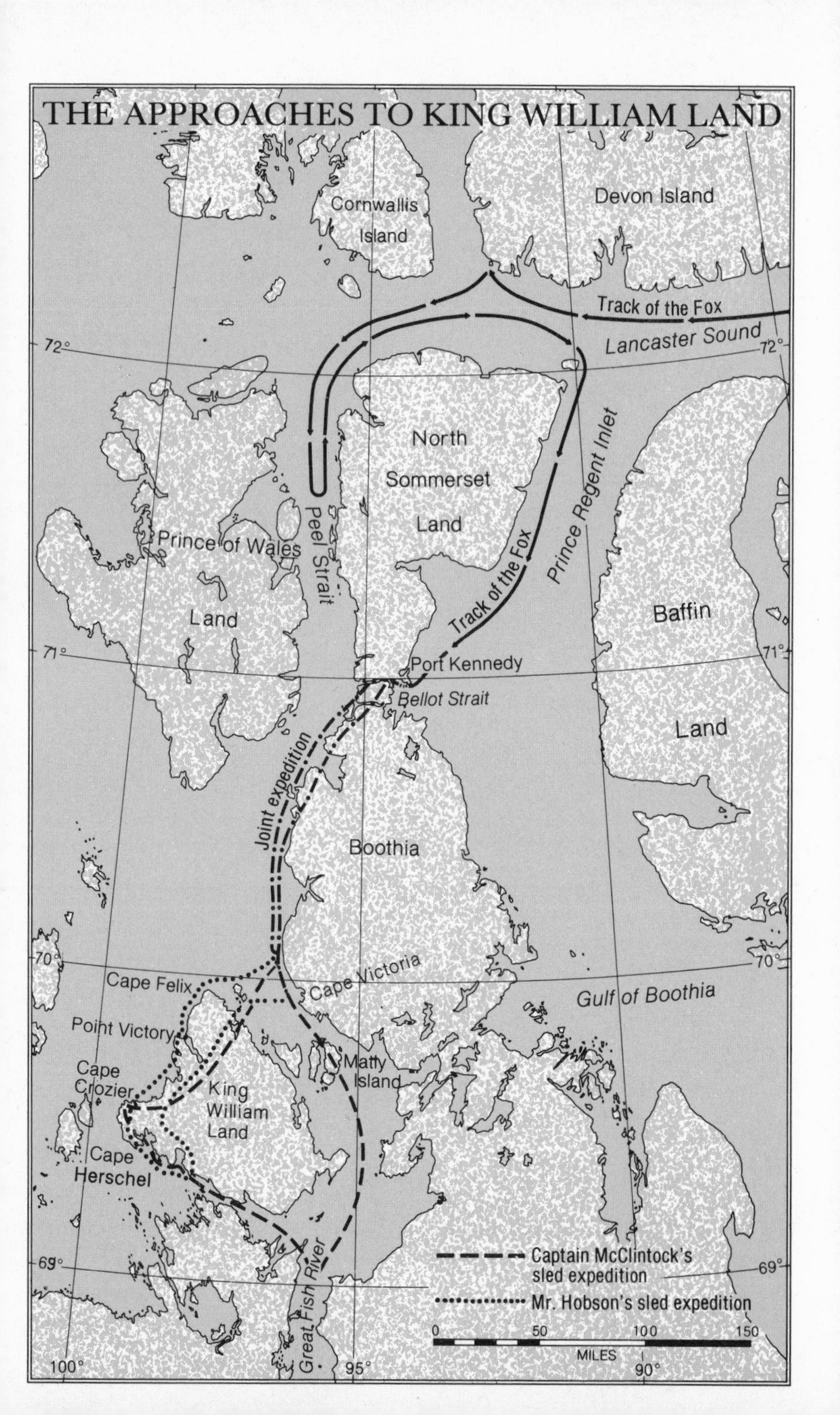

THE APPROACHES TO KING WILLIAM LAND
Cornwallis Island
Devon Island
Track of the Fox
Lancaster Sound
72°
North Sommerset Land
Prince Regent Inlet
Peel Strait
Prince of Wales Land
Track of the Fox
Baffin Land
71°
Port Kennedy
Bellot Strait
Joint expedition
Boothia
70°
Cape Felix
Cape Victoria
Gulf of Boothia
Point Victory
Matty Island
Cape Crozier
King William Land
Cape Herschel
Great Fish River
69°
Captain McClintock's sled expedition
Mr. Hobson's sled expedition
0
50
100
150
MILES
100°
95°
90°

FOREWORD

This account of the last voyage in the long search for Sir John Franklin is based on Captain Leopold McClintock's *The Voyage of the Fox in the Arctic Seas* (London, 1859).

Sir John Franklin sailed for the Arctic in 1845 with two ships, *Erebus* and *Terror,* and 128 officers and men in an attempt to complete the work of earlier explorers by navigating the Northwest Passage. The eastern approaches to the passage had been explored and the continental shore had been mapped westward from Boothia to the Bering Strait. Between these known areas lay some three hundred uncharted miles. Franklin's orders were to cross that gap by sea and so to complete the passage.

When, after three years, no news of the expedition had been received, a rescue party was sent out. This was the first of more than forty such expeditions; thousands of miles in the Arctic regions were searched for traces of the missing ships. Only the information obtained by Dr. John Rae from the Boothian Eskimos seemed to offer any clue as to what had happened. In 1856 the British Government refused to support any further attempt.

It was at this point that Lady Franklin, despairing of any official help, set about organizing her own expedition. The 177-ton *Fox* was bought and equipped for Arctic service. The command was offered to Leopold McClintock, a veteran of three previous search parties.

The expedition was out for two years. Shortly after its return in 1859, McClintock's narrative was published. It provides a detailed account of the voyage—its progress, setbacks, and achievements. It lists the officers of the *Fox,* the Danish interpreter, the two Greenland Eskimos, and the ship's company of eighteen men. To some of the latter, fictitious names have been assigned, and to one of them, the youngest of the able-bodied seamen, has been given the role of narrator. The substance of his story is, however, not fiction but a matter of record.

Aloft we all must go-oh,
John come down the backstay,
In hail and frost and snow-oh,
John come down the backstay,
John Dameray!

Sea chantey

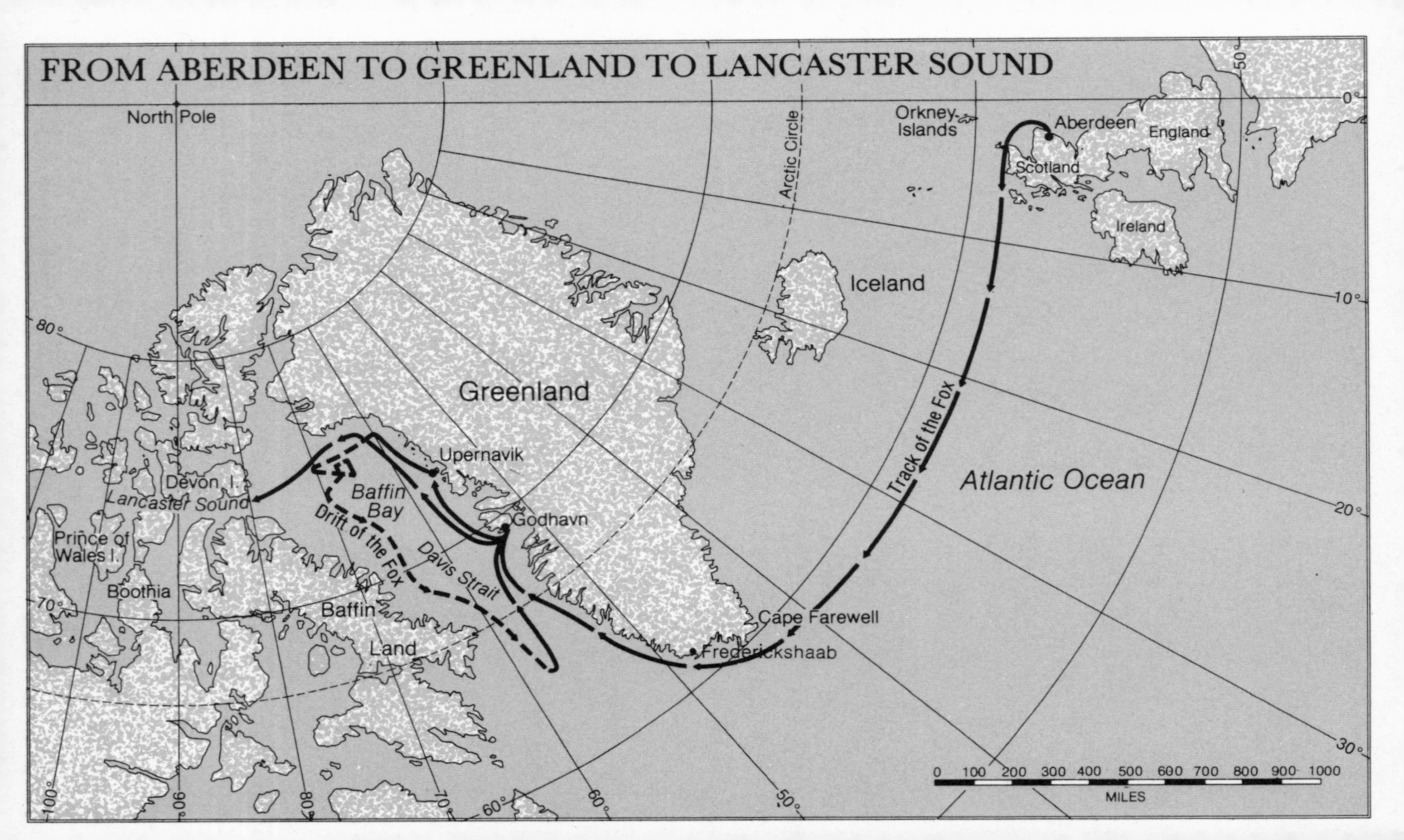

FROM ABERDEEN TO GREENLAND TO LANCASTER SOUND
North Pole
Arctic Circle
Orkney Islands
Aberdeen
England
Scotland
Ireland
Iceland
Greenland
Track of the Fox
Atlantic Ocean
Upernavik
Devon I.
Lancaster Sound
Baffin Bay
Drift of the Fox
Godhavn
Prince of Wales I.
Davis Strait
Boothia
Baffin Land
Cape Farewell
Frederickshaab
0 100 200 300 400 500 600 700 800 900 1000
MILES

June 29, 1857

ABERDEEN

We sail tomorrow, or so the Captain says. It doesn't seem likely to me. We've been loading the *Fox* for a week, and the wharf is still piled high with gear waiting to be stowed. The deck is a shambles, barrels and boxes and bundles everywhere. Below decks there's hardly room to put down a seabag, much less the clothes and medicines and scientific instruments that have to be packed in somewhere. At least the stores are safely aboard: pemmican by the thousands of pounds, ale by the dozens of barrels, lemon juice, vegetables in brine, pickles, and great dumpy bags of sugar and flour.

The ice gear went on board today. There are saws with teeth that could rip the flesh from the bone if you should happen to run your hand across them the wrong way, kegs of powder for blasting a channel through the ice, coils of fuse, and jagged anchors and ice claws. All these pieces of equipment are strange to me but old friends to most of the crew. Listening to them talk, I'd guess that more than half the men have served in the Arctic before.

At the far end of the wharf, like fashionable ladies who have lost their way home, are the *Fox*'s old fittings —velvet curtains, mahogany bunks, mirrors, and the elegant little brass propellor that used to take her on summer cruises through the Mediterranean. No more easy voyages for the *Fox*. Her new propellor is heavy and businesslike. Her hull is "doubled" and the prow is sheeted so thick in iron that it looks like a great blunt hatchet. Beams and crosspieces strengthen her sides and fresh planks glare yellow on the decks where the hatches and skylights have been narrowed against foul weather and the cold.

One of the skylights is almost directly over my bunk. I'm lucky in this, because most of the fo'c'sle is dark. There are hurricane lamps, of course, with their warm smell of kerosene and soot, but I have sunlight and moonlight as well. I'm pleased with my bunk. It is right up in the bow, built against the heavy oak stem-post. Although it's an upper bunk, there is space to sling a small catchall hammock over it, so I have room for books, pens, and paper and ink and the box of "assortments." "Assortments" is Mother's word; I don't care for it but have never been able to think of a better one. I suppose it was foolish to bring the box. What use will I find in the Arctic for the old silver florin that I found in a crack in the washhouse floor, or for the tail of the first rabbit I shot, or for any of the other things? But I'm glad I brought it, all the same. In the hammock, too, there is a package marked "Do not open until December 25, 1857." Another one, labeled for 1858, is safe at the bottom of my sea chest.

Mr. Hobson joined the ship today as second in command. It was good to see him again, a familiar face. I went down to the wharf to help him carry up his bags. I wanted to thank him for recommending me to Captain McClintock, but he cut me short. "It was nothing, nothing at all." I tried again. "I really am grateful, sir. Half the boys in the Navy asked for leave to go on this expedition, and it is owing to you . . ." "It was nothing," he said again and started up the gangway. Old Harvey, the quartermaster, showed him to his cabin, and I followed along with the bags. The officers' quarters are almost as cramped as ours. Apart from the bunk and the lockers under it, there's only room in the cabin for a wall-hung desk, a straight chair, and a shelf. A big man like Mr. Hobson can hardly square his shoulders in such a pigeonhole.

Visitors from the town have been on and off the ship all day, poking around, getting in the way, asking questions. "Doesn't it make you giddy to be up there in the rigging?" "Won't you miss your family on such a long voyage?" "Do you get seasick?" They meant kindly, but after a while I began to get angry. I wanted to answer them, "I'm not a green hand. I know what I'm doing or I wouldn't be here." But I managed to hold my tongue. There was one question, though, of an entirely different kind. "The *Fox* is very small for such an undertaking, don't you think?" It was an old man with a sailor's wide-legged walk who asked that. I couldn't answer him; I wondered about it myself. How will the *Fox* take to the ice and winds of the far north? They say that the pack ice can crush even a man-o'-war like an old basket and that the best canvas is no better than tissue paper in those gales. And the *Fox* is narrow-beamed and small, not much over a hundred feet long.

Lady Franklin comes tomorrow to inspect her ship. I wonder what she'll think of her little *Fox*.

June 30
ABERDEEN

Early this morning, well before daybreak, we were at work stowing the last of the gear. Because I'm the smallest and youngest hand on board, everyone from the Captain to the carpenter's mate claimed me as his own particular messenger boy. At times they had me running a dozen errands at once. Along the wharf to the stores for an extra packet of needles for the sailmaker, off to the inn with the Captain's letters for London, down to the hold to make sure that the dogsleds were lashed securely, back to the galley to count yeast cakes. On one of these errands, I don't know which, I lost my knife. It was a good knife, too, with a dark horn handle banded in silver, two blades, and a spike.

By noon, everything was in its place and the *Fox* scrubbed and ready to be off. She looked very smart, dressed in all her flags, with fresh paint gleaming and the brass the soft clear yellow of recent polishing. I changed into my new jacket, tried to flatten down my hair, and then went and stood with the others by the rail. The Captain came up. "Any sign of Lady Franklin?" he asked. "No, sir, not yet." "This will not be an easy day for her ladyship," he said. "I want you all to spare her as much distress as you can." "How do you mean, sir?" "It has been twelve years now since her husband sailed for the Arctic with the *Erebus* and the *Terror*," the Captain said slowly. "For all those years she has not known whether he was alive or dead, if he succeeded in finding the Northwest Passage, or if he failed. The Admiralty sent out ships to look for him. Some of you men took part in those expeditions, I believe." "That's right, sir," said several voices. "You know, then, that no trace was ever found of the missing ships except a deserted camp on a remote island." "Beechey Island," said someone in agreement. "The Admiralty gave up the search, refusing to risk any more lives in what they termed a futile effort. But Lady Franklin was convinced that one more attempt should be made to find her husband and the brave men who sailed with him. She organized this expedition to make that final effort. So I think you can understand how she will feel today." We nodded, subdued by what he had said. But I know that we were all confident that we would succeed where the others had failed and bring Sir John Franklin and the men of the *Erebus* and *Terror* triumphantly home to England.

Shortly after that, Lady Franklin arrived. She is shorter than I had imagined, stouter and not as handsome as she looks in the newspaper drawings. But then, the drawings give no hint of the energy and determination that you notice at once when you see her. The languid beauty in *The Illustrated London News* could never have assembled this expedition. She was wearing a cloak with a thick border of fur—fox fur perhaps. If it was, it was a nice touch.

The boatswain's pipe shrilled. We lined up, stiff as posts, and stared up at the yards in proper Navy fashion. It was soon clear, though, that this was no formal inspection and we all relaxed. Lady Franklin went through her ship like a woman in a new house. She sat on the bunks to see if the mattresses were soft, admired the oil-burning stoves that will be used to heat the ship in the winter, and even tried a few notes on Rob Harmsworth's accordion. "I'm afraid I don't play very well," she said. "It's not an easy instrument for a lady, ma'am," answered Rob, glancing at her shyly under his thick dark brows. She spent some time in the boiler room, but far more in the galley. Seeing the neat stacks of yeast cakes that I had counted in the morning, she smiled. "I shall think with pleasure of the smell of fresh-baked bread floating from the *Fox* and away over the ice." There was a shaking in her voice, but she steadied it at once. Then she looked at me. "You were a babe in arms when my husband sailed," she said suddenly. I was completely taken aback. I tried to say something, but I could feel the salt water coming into my eyes and I wasn't sorry when she turned away.

The harbor master came on board and told the Captain that we should sail within the hour if we wanted to catch the tide. We all gathered on deck, and Lady Franklin shook hands with each one of us and wished us well. Then, even though the Captain was glaring at us, we called for "Three cheers for Lady Franklin!" and gave them heartily. She walked down the gangway with a handkerchief to her eyes, but she must have been pleased, all the same, and we could see that the Captain was pleased too. The last of the visitors and the wives and friends of the crew followed her ashore. I had no one to wave to, having said my good-byes days ago in Lowestoft, and was glad when at last the *Fox* was cast off. A dozen small boys, barefoot and with their trousers rolled above their knees, raced us out along the pier, waving and shouting. Looking back, I could make out a dash of red on the wharf: Lady Franklin's cape. The *Fox*'s foghorn gave a long blast, a parting salute, and we steamed out toward the open sea.

The ship began to pitch gently, catching the swell. The wind was fresh and I tasted salt on my tongue. I thought, We're off. But then, changing course, the *Fox* swung round faster than the helmsman had anticipated. She faltered, as if a giant hand had reached up from the bottom and caught her by the keel, and settled firmly on the harbor bar. So here we are, with the lights of Aberdeen on the bow, waiting for the tide to float us off. What a beginning!

We slipped off the bar on the early morning tide. The town was still asleep and only a few fishermen saw us go.

The watches were chosen this morning in the traditional Navy way. Mr. Young, the sailing master, picked first, and then Mr. Hobson. Rob and the red-haired Scot, Alec Macrae, were among the first to be chosen, I noticed. I was the last.

After weeks of waking days and uninterrupted nights, it will be hard to get used to the pattern of ship's life again. Four hours on, four hours off, with the two-hour dogwatch as a half step to break the rhythm. Tonight we have the graveyard watch, the hardest of all to turn out for, even when you've been at sea for months. One thing to be thankful for, though, is that my stomach is steady. We're only five men to a watch, and there's no time for anyone to hang over the side feeling green. Even so, Raydon Jones, who is the oldest man on our watch though not the senior, is never too busy to come round after me checking my work. And I can feel eyes on me whenever I'm aloft. It makes me bristle.

July 3

Last night we battled our way through the Pentland Firth, tide and wind fighting each other and the *Fox* struggling with both. In the half-darkness the noise was overwhelming—the crash and rush of the water, the incessant high shriek of the wind in the rigging, the screaming of thousands and thousands of unseen birds. When I went below, Alec Macrae, his sandy hair like flame in the lamplight, was telling over the names of the ships that went down in the Firth last winter. "The barque *Melissa,* all hands lost . . . the pilot-ship *Erith*. She was from Ronaldsay, see, and the crew all Orkney men. Wrecked on their own rocks. Then there was the *Nan Storrs* . . . the *Bonnie Lass*. . ." The names of the drowned ships and the noise of the storm wheeled round and round in my head and for a long time I couldn't get to sleep.

July 4

The last of the Orkney Islands is over the horizon and we are making for Greenland, bowling along under a cloud of canvas, as the old sailors say. It is a comparatively small cloud—the *Fox* carries nothing above the topgallants—but we're making good speed all the same.

I was dreadfully thirsty all through the afternoon watch, probably because I put salt on my potatoes at dinner, when they were already well seasoned. Afterward I went to the galley to get a billy of water, and there was my knife lying on a pile of peelings. The blade was stained and rusty but the handle with its silver band was unmistakable. I forgot all about the water and stood leaning against the bulkhead, wondering what to say. Cooky was busy with some mixture in a big bowl, stirring it roughly and muttering under his breath. He seemed in a bad mood. Eventually I said, "I had a knife exactly like that one, but I lost it." He clicked his tongue. "Pity," he said. "I lost it the day we sailed." His round white face was inscrutable. Did he think that I was accusing him of stealing the knife? To my relief he laughed. "Found it under the stove yesterday," he said. "It ain't mine. Might well be yours." He wiped off the potato juice with a corner of his apron, flicked the blade over the whetstone, and passed the knife to me. I thanked him and started back for the fo'c'sle. He called after me, "Hey! Wait a minute." "Yes?" " 'Ungry, are you? Boys! Feed them three good meals a day and they're still starvin'." "No," I said, remembering, "I wanted some water to make tea." He filled the billy and then gave me a piece of gingerbread left over from the officers' dinner. "Now, don't you come round 'ere beggin' all the time," he said, but he was grinning.

Tonight I carved five notches in the post at the head of my bunk, one for each day of the voyage. Steve Smith watched me closely as I did it, but he didn't say anything. He seldom does, nor does his brother, Sy. Rob Harmsworth calls them "The Silent Smiths," as if they were an act in the circus! Both of them are stokers by trade. Perhaps that's why they are so quiet: you can't talk to a heap of coal.

July 6

The wind is still with us, the sun is hot, and from horizon to horizon there's not a cloud, just a blue spread of sky above a shining blue ocean. Captain McClintock read the Sunday service on deck, standing at the foot of the mainmast with the officers and Mr. Brands, the engineer. I hadn't noticed before how dark the Captain's eyes are, as black as the *Fox*'s hull and put in with a sooty finger, like so many Irishmen's.

After the service, the Captain took a folded paper out of his prayer book. "Before we sailed," he said, "Lady Franklin gave me a packet, which I was not to open until we were fairly out in the Atlantic. It contained her instructions for this expedition. I thought that I should share her words with you." He unfolded the paper. "She writes, 'As to the objects of this expedition and their relative importance, I am sure you know that the rescue of any possible survivor of the *Erebus* and *Terror* would be to me, as it would be to you, the noblest result of our efforts. Next in importance is the recovery of the documents of the expedition. Lastly, I hope that you may be able to confirm the claims of my husband's expedition to the earliest discovery of the Northwest Passage.' " He glanced up from the paper. "She ends by saying that her fear is that we may spend ourselves too much in the effort and that our safe return is more important to her than anything else." He paused, looking around at the men. "For myself," he said, "I would consider no effort too great, in such a cause."

He dismissed us. We walked aft and stood looking back along the *Fox*'s wake, straight as a string stretched across the ocean. "There is a man, if ever there was one, who will not turn back until he has finished what he set out to do," said James Pride, the second engineer. "You never said a truer word," agreed Old Harvey. "He's not the kind that would ever turn his back on trouble, not while he still had a face to face it with."

July 8

This morning the sky was overcast and the wind rising. Even in my bunk I could feel the *Fox* strain as she raced along. Pulling my oilskins out of my sea chest was far from easy. The ship was pitching and the lid of the chest kept trying to slam itself shut on my fingers.

When I got on deck—late—Mr. Hobson was timing

the log line as it whipped out over the rail. We stood by, waiting. "Shorten sail," he said at last, turning the sandglass over. We took in the fore-topsail. Rob lay out along the yard first. For all his bulk, he is very agile. If there is anyone in the ship who can hang on with his belly muscles and his eyebrows, as the clipper men say, it is Rob. He shouted, "Keep your eyes on your hands and don't look down!" I could barely hear him for the wind. I looked down, in spite of myself. There was nothing below me but the heaving sea. I swung out and down toward it, while my fingers scrabbled and slid on the yard, feeling for a grip. Out and down and down. The *Fox* plunged and shuddered and started to swing back. The deck was under me and then there was gray sky and a blow of rain in my face. I shut my eyes. The footrope shook as Rob worked his way along the yard toward me. "Don't you know any better than that?" he said roughly and hooked his arm around mine. We inched back to the security of the shrouds, then down to the greater security of the deck. The others reefed the main-topsail. The straining eased.

In the fo'c'sle the stove was glowing and someone had rigged up a spider's web of a clothesline. Socks and sweaters hung from it, steaming. The air was thick with the smell of onions frying and wet wool and sweet tobacco smoke. The men wrapped their hands around mugs of hot tea, everyone warm and happy—except me. I know I should have thanked Rob, but I couldn't even look him in the eye. What he doesn't understand is that I *do* know better than to look down from the yards.

July 9

I am worried about Dick Singleton. Ever since we left Aberdeen he has been coughing, coughing, coughing. Today he got up, stood swaying for a second or two, and then sat down abruptly on his bunk with his head in his hands. He coughed–hard–and lay back. "Will you do me a favor?" he asked. "Of course," I said. "I don't feel too well, but I don't want anyone to find out. I know you just came below, but could you work my watch for me? I'll be better later on." "Of course," I said again and slid my hands back down my wet sleeves.

It was still blowing hard, though not as hard as it had been earlier, and the rain was sheeting down. Weather like this makes everything twice as difficult. I pulled my sou'wester down until it hid my face and reported to Mr. Young, the officer of the starboard watch. He sent me up aloft to check the ratlines. It was a slow, tedious business and occupied me for the whole of the watch. If anyone noticed that it wasn't Dick working up there, he kept his peace. Then it was my watch again. Mr. Hobson gave me the wheel. "Keep her as she is." By the end of the watch, I was hanging on to the spokes to keep myself upright, I was so tired. Twelve hours running in the cold rain and the wind!

When at last I went below, Dick was restless. "How do you feel?" I asked him. "It's the cough, you see," he said. "It tears me apart. But the salt air will do me good. Salt air will cure anything." He gave a weak little laugh, which turned into a cough mid-way. "Thank you for today," he said, when he got his breath again. "Don't worry about it, Dick. Don't worry about it." I rolled onto my bunk fully dressed, too exhausted to ask if he had found someone to stand in for him for the next watch.

July 10

"Rise and shine!" I slid off my bunk more than half asleep. Then I looked at Dick and came awake with a jerk. He was drenched with sweat and there was a trickle of blood at the corner of his mouth. I ran for Doctor Walker. My legs were shaking. The Doctor looked at Dick and listened as he coughed and coughed as if he would never stop. "Stay with him until I get back," he said. I sat on the edge of Dick's bunk; I was still shaking and didn't want him to see it. When the Doctor returned, Captain McClintock was with him. "We will have to get you back to England, Singleton," he said. "Warmth and sunlight are what those lungs of yours need, not two years in the Arctic." Dick looked at him wretchedly and tried to say something, but the cough tore at him again and he only nodded. They moved him into the small spare cabin that the doctor calls his hospital.

A heavy sea is running, rolling down from before the port beam, and the *Fox* is plunging like a seesaw.

Up—and she stands on her stern. Down—and she crashes into the wave trough, hurling out white wings of spray. The plunge and recoil shake her through her entire length. It's a challenge to move around. I shall be black and blue tomorrow, but I've enjoyed it. For Dick, slamming from side to side in his bunk in the hospital, it must be misery.

July 12

The wind has taken off considerably, and this forenoon Mr. Hobson ordered all sail set again. I went aloft with the others. My hands were sweating and the blood was like a drum in my ears, but I didn't look down.

Rob slid down on the main-topmast backstay, landing on deck as neatly as a dancer while the rest of us were still hand-over-handing it in the shrouds. One day I'll find the nerve to do that.

July 13

Yesterday's moderate wind has dropped to a mere breeze, so today was given over to housekeeping. Extra water was issued for laundering clothes, and all the bedding was hung on the rail to air. My clothes came out of the bucket in various shades of gray. White shirts turned pale gray, underwear yellow gray, and socks an odd shade of oil gray. But at least the salt is out of them, and they are softer now.

It is strange how, when one dislikes someone, small irritations grow out of all proportion. Raydon Jones's double sniff, for example. "Nff, nff." If anyone else sniffed like that, I'd probably not even notice.

Raydon chivvies me all day long. "Look sharp now . . . hurry up . . . be quick . . . your hands are filthy. What kind of impression do you think you make on Mr. Hobson, looking like that? . . . Nff, nff . . . I know your kind, always cutting corners." On and on. I have told myself at least a dozen times that he is an old man and set in his ways, and I've tried to convince myself that he finds me just as irritating as I find him. But it's no good. I hear that "nff, nff," and my jaw muscles clench. We share the same watch, we share the same table, we share everything. We'll be sharing them two years from now. For two years it will be nag, nag, and "nff, nff." I don't think I'll be able to stand it.

I dreamed about Raydon the other night. I was in some kind of a cage, big enough to move around in but with no door. The bars were halyards, badly worn, and the floor was black with dirt. There was a holystone, a bucket of water, and an unspeakable rag in one corner of the cage. And Raydon walked round and round outside, with his little eyes blinking and his sharp nose twitching. He looked like a mouse, but I was the one in the trap.

July 15

Most sailors like to spin a yarn and have a couple of good stories to tell when the mood strikes them, but with the old Arctic hands on the *Fox,* telling stories is like breathing. They are always at it, Rob and James Pride, Old Harvey and Alec and Dusty Miller, all of them. (All Millers are "Dusty" in the Navy, and usually the nickname seems appropriate. This Dusty, though, is a thin man with a sallow skin and a long upper lip like a horse's. "Dusty" is all wrong for him, but no one seems to know what his real name is.)

This passion for telling stories has been puzzling me for some time, and today I asked Rob about it. "Use your head now," he said. "Think of those long winter days and nights. The sun never comes over the horizon. The ships are fast in the ice. The only light is a smoky lantern. If a man doesn't know how to read or knit or crochet, what can he do but tell stories?" When he mentioned knitting and crocheting, I laughed, but he said reprovingly, "Some of the men do work that would put their womenfolk to shame. I remember old Abbott. He was with the *Pioneer* and I was on the *Assistance.* That was in '50 and '51. He made a shawl for his wife and one for each of his three daughters. Fine, fine work, and each shawl a different pattern." I nodded, trying to be properly appreciative of the old sailor's skill, but still finding it a little comic.

"Hey, Harvey," Rob called out. "Do you remember Abbott? And the shawls?" "Abbott? I'll never forget him." Old Harvey walked over stiffly—his joints seize up when the wind is northerly, he says—and eased himself onto someone's sea chest. "Do you remember the bear?" "What bear?" I asked, and thought, Another story, he has that look to him. "Well," said Old Harvey, "We were up by the Devil's Thumb in Melville Bay. The Captain wanted some of us to take a boat ashore and shoot loons. So off we went, with a gun apiece and four pounds of bird shot. Then we saw the bear, a big old fellow, pacing up and down on an island offshore, looking for a seal for his dinner, I daresay. We forgot all about the loons and started to shoot at him. We shot as fast as we could load the guns, and all that happened was that the bear shrugged his shoulders and twitched his skin, like a horse that's bothered with flies. Oh, it made me angry! So I took an old knife and cut a button off my coat and rammed the knife and the button together down the barrel. The knife caught him in the flank, you could see the blood on his fur. He jumped in the water and started to swim away. Abbott yelled, 'Come on, mates, we've got him now!' and we rowed after him. When we were almost on him, the bear pulled himself up onto a piece of ice and started snarling at us and hitting out with his front paws. Abbott was in the prow with a boat hook, all ready to grab at the bear, yelling 'Pull! Pull!' Some of the men did pull, but the rest of us thought better of it—I tell you, it was the biggest bear I've ever seen, and the angriest—and we backed oars. So the boat spun around and the bear floated off on his piece of ice, laughing at us, I swear. Abbott said that if we hadn't been such cowards, he'd have brought the bear back to the ship and trained it to pull a sled!" "And all that winter, if anyone grumbled at the weight of the sleds, Abbott would say, 'It's your own fault. If you'd taken my advice, we'd have had that there bear to do the work for us,' " added Rob, smiling.

I hoped that they would go on telling stories of bear hunts, but they were off on a different tack. "What a winter that was!" Rob said. "All those ships at Beechey Island. The *Assistance* and the *Resolute* and the *Pioneer*. The *Felix* and Captain Penney's two brigs. And the Americans with *Advance* and *Rescue*." "Yes," said Old Harvey, "that was the year. 'The great search for Franklin,' they called it. And it was a great search, too, though all we found was that camp on Beechey Island." "It gave me a strange feeling, that camp," said Rob, reflectively. "Look, I'm not a fanciful man, but think of it. Franklin had been there, only four years before us. The markers on those graves proved it. Two men from the *Erebus*, one from the *Terror*, dead and buried in 1846. I'll never forget those graves. And Franklin and his ships had gone without a trace. Somehow I had the feeling that the same might happen to us." "I know what you mean," said Old Harvey. "Do you remember that pair of gloves I found there? No, I don't suppose you do. They were old gloves, worn right through on the thumb and first finger of the right hand. It must have been a warm day, and the gloves too clumsy for the work he was doing. He took them off and put a stone on them, so that the wind wouldn't blow them away. And then . . . what happened then?"

July 16

We are in the ice! I woke and heard it grating and rasping along the *Fox*'s hull within a foot or two of my head. I scrambled into my clothes, rushed on deck, and stood there blinking. The pack surrounds us from horizon to horizon. I had thought that it would be like the ice on the fens, slick and gray and flat. It's quite different. It's a ruined city, rough broken blocks piled up in towers and walls or crushed into rubble. And blindingly white in the sun.

At deck level the ice seems very dense, but you can see open lanes of water—"leads," they call them—if you go up to the crow's nest. Mr. Hobson sent me up to watch Rob. "You are new to the ice," he said. "You can learn a lot from Harmsworth. He was born aboard a whaler, or so he says, and his first words were 'Thar she blows!' " He laughed. "Well, be that as it may, he certainly has an uncanny knowledge of the ice. You will learn more in an hour watching him than you would in a week studying a textbook, if there were one." I climbed up the shrouds and perched on the fore-topsail yard. There's only room for one in the *Fox*'s crow's nest, a barrel lashed to the foremast head. Rob was standing in the barrel, his elbows on the rim and his hands shading his eyes. I could just see the snaky tail of the dragon he has tattooed on his right arm. "Steady as you are," he shouted. Someone below echoed him, calling back to the man at the wheel, "Steady as you are."

Ahead of us, open water wound dark between the ice floes to the middle distance. There an iceberg lay across the lead, blocking our way. We sailed steadily on with the wind on the beam. As we got closer, I could see that the iceberg was not white, as I'd thought, but pale green where the sun struck it and purple and blue in the shadows. It was rather like an enormous mushroom with a ragged overhanging cap. "Two degrees a' port," shouted Rob, and the order was repeated below. I said, "Aren't we turning too soon?" and wished at once that I could bite off my tongue. Rob didn't look round; he just shrugged. The ship started to turn. The sails hung limp, then slowly filled on the new course, and the *Fox* swung round neatly well clear of the berg. It took our wind and for a moment we hung in the open water in its lee, feeling the chill.

I stayed on the yard for the whole of the watch, studying the path of open water ahead, trying to judge the steering and the timing of the orders shouted down to the helmsman. When there was a turn in the lead, I silently gave the new course. By the end of the four-hour stint, some of my unspoken orders coincided with Rob's. "Getting the hang of it?" he asked as we clambered stiffly down to the deck. "It takes practice and a good eye and knowing your ship to bring her cleanly through the ice. Practice most of all."

July 17

Still in the ice. Alec Macrae says that this is nothing compared with the heavy pack waiting for us in the north. "You think I'm fooling," he said, sliding one sandy eyebrow up his forehead almost to the roots of his hair. "Well, you'll see. This is child's play. I mean it."

On the forenoon watch, I asked Mr. Hobson if I could go aloft again with Rob. "So you're ambitious to be an ice-master?" he asked, teasing me. "No, not really, sir, but . . ." I couldn't explain to him the feeling of freedom and power that I had had up there in the yards yesterday. "There's nothing much to be done on deck," he said. "I think we could spare you."

I spent most of that watch perched on the yard above Rob's head. The ice was looser than it had been yesterday and the main trend of the lead was confused by side channels twisting away into the pack. But we could see clear to the horizon and "gentled her through, nice and easy," as Rob said afterwards.

July 18

It was the brush and pail and "swab her down" for me this morning, a job I hate. I finished in double-quick time and asked permission to join Rob in the crow's nest for the rest of the watch. Mr. Hobson looked surprised, but the deck was spotless and he let me go.

Up there, above the shadow of the sails, the sun was brilliant. Rob's eyes were screwed up against its glare, pulling his whole face out of shape. He gave me a crooked grin. After a while he said, "Alright now, take her around that next bend." The lead swung off to starboard in the first curve of a giant *S*. I brought the *Fox* successfully around. Rob nodded his approval and I called down the orders that turned gradually to port and completed the figure. It was as if I had the *Fox* on the end of a string like a toy boat in a pond. "Not bad, not bad at all," he said. I could have cheered! "Look," he went on, "I'm going down to get a hat. Might help keep the sun off. You'll be alright on your own?" "Of course," I answered confidently. He disappeared through the trapdoor in the bottom of the crow's nest and I slid down into his place. The obedient little *Fox* was mine.

He had been gone the best part of an hour when I saw the iceberg ahead, lying low and massive in the water. I looked down; there was no sign of Rob. Well, I had taken the bends of the *S* by myself. We got closer to the berg. I could see pools of water on its slopes, where its snowy coat had been melted by the sun. "Hard a' port," I shouted down. The ship started to turn, but slowly, slowly. I had left it too late. "Hard a' port!" My voice sounded strange, very thin and shrill. Rob was racing up the shrouds. Too late. One great arm of the berg reached out for us. There was a shudder and the sound of splintering wood.

I climbed shakily down to the deck. All the officers were there and most of the men. Even Dick Singleton had been hurried up from his hospital berth at the shock of the collision. All those eyes watched me come down.

July 19

The damage is not as bad as I had thought. There are three broken planks, all of them above the waterline.

I reported to Mr. Hobson. He looked at me grimly. "The crow's nest, I think, don't you?" It wasn't a question; it was an order. I climbed up and settled in the barrel, very alert and very miserable. Then the fog rolled in as sudden and total as if the door to a lighted room had been closed, leaving us in the dark passage outside. Iceberg shapes loomed ahead. My breath was gathered in, ready to give the warning, but as we reached them the shapes dissolved and were gone. Then the wind died and there was a strange, damp silence. The shrouds creaked as someone climbed up. His head came in view, hooded and scarfed in fog. It was Mr. Hobson. "Fog!" he said. "How I hate it. Some of the old sailors will tell you that you can hear the voices of drowned children in the fog. Don't you believe it." I didn't believe it, but I was glad of his company all the same.

The fog lifted this evening as suddenly as it had come. Shortly after, we cleared the last of the ice. The coast of Greenland was on the horizon, snow-covered and glowing pink in the sunset. Alec began to sing the hymn about "Greenland's icy mountains." His voice is surprisingly sweet, with that piercing quality that sends responsive shivers down your spine. Rob picked up the tune on his accordion and we sang with him. Then Dusty asked for "Lady Franklin's Lament." I hadn't heard it before.

'Twas homeward bound one night on the deep,
Slung in my hammock fast asleep,
I had a dream, which I thought was true,
Concerning Franklin and his bold crew.

'Twas as we near'd the English shore,
I heard a lady sadly deplore;
She wept aloud, and seemed to say,
"Alas my husband is long away.

"In Baffin Bay where the whale-fish blows,
Is the fate of Franklin—no one knows.
Ten thousand pounds would I freely give,
To learn that my husband still did live. . . ."

After they finished the song, Rob went on playing, drawing out those long sighing notes that only an accordion can produce.

July 20

FREDERICKSHAAB

Early this morning a boat came off to us from the shore. It turned out that it belonged to the Danish governor of Frederickshaab, who had sent his pilot to guide us into the harbor. The mail ship calls here. Dick is to take the ship to Copenhagen and then get passage home to London.

After we had everything neatly squared away, the Captain ordered a boat lowered. James Pride and I were told to row him ashore. For someone who spends most of his time with engines, James handles a boat remarkably well. He has a fisherman's easy swing with an oar. Halfway to the landing place, we found we had an escort: a dozen or more Eskimo kayaks. They moved so fast that our boat seemed to stand still in the water, even though we were rowing as hard as we could. The Eskimos shouted something to us. James called back to them, and they laughed. "What did you say to them?" I asked when the Captain had gone ashore. "I said 'Good-day.' It's the only word I know." "Then why were they laughing?" "I imagine I sound very odd. It's harder than you might think to get your tongue around those consonants. It took me a whole day to learn that one word."

While we were waiting for the Captain, I had a chance to look at one of the kayaks drawn up on the shingle beach. It seemed terribly fragile, nothing but a sealskin cover stretched over a narrow frame of drift-wood. James seemed to know something about the

Eskimos, so I asked him, "Do they use the kayaks in the winter, too? There must be a lot of ice in the water then and if one of these hit ice, there'd be no saving it." "Yes," he said, "but they seldom hit. Watch that boy out there." One of the kayaks was still out in the harbor, making circles around the *Fox*. I could see how quick and responsive it was. One flick of the paddle and it turned. As I was watching, the Eskimo gave too strong a stroke and tipped right over. He came up spluttering and laughing in the icy water, righted his boat, and climbed back in. James said, "He's just a boy, with a lot to learn," and glanced at me. But his voice was friendly; Raydon's, when he makes that kind of a remark, has a sour edge to it. "Did you ever read about the Centaurs, half man and half horse?" James asked. "When an Eskimo is hunting at sea, he is half man and half boat. The kayak is so completely under his control that it seems like an extension of his body."

James is a strange kind of person to find among the fo'c'sle hands. He is more like a schoolmaster than a sailor, with his lined forehead and his beaky nose. He talks like a book, too.

July 21

Jackson, the carpenter, started work on the broken planks, hanging over the side on a rope sling. I offered to help. He muttered something about "done enough damage," so I went away.

Rob and James and I rowed across to the river mouth, where the Eskimos have a camp for the summer fishing. There was no one in sight. Rows of trout were strung up in the sun, some of them dried and brown, some still silvery fresh. There must be as many as twenty tents in the camp. They are made of some kind of skin, stretched and scraped so that it is almost transparent. We looked in one. In the dusky orange light we could just make out a pile of fishing tackle and a huddle of furs on a platform at the back. The furs moved, and we saw that there was an old woman there, fast asleep. At least, I think she was asleep. I hope she was. We dropped the door flap, feeling very large and foreign and foolish.

July 22

The mail ship, with Dick aboard, sailed today, and we will sail tomorrow. I'll be glad to be gone. Frederickshaab is a pleasant enough little port, I suppose, rather like a north-country village set down in a landscape of glaciers. But for me Frederickshaab will always be Dick coming along the wharf with the fever bright in his face and me sideslipping away between the houses to avoid him. Why? It would have been so easy just to smile and say, "Good-bye, Dick. Good luck." Why couldn't I do it?

July 28

Feelings ran very high in the fo'c'sle tonight. It all started, strangely enough, with a pair of mittens. James bought them from a trader in Frederickshaab, real Eskimo mittens, beautifully made of sealskin with a border of fine white fur around the cuffs. James put one of them on and handed the other to me. "What do you think of this?" he asked. I suppose that it was because it was so bulky on my hand that the mitten reminded me of the puppets Mother used to make me out of Uncle Dan's worn-out socks. I turned the mitten toward James and made it bow hesitantly. "Agloochick?" I said in a high voice, trying to sound like an Eskimo. James understood immediately. His mitten lunged at mine, a fierce hunter pursuing a reluctant girl. I gave a little giggling shriek and made my mitten mince away from his. He lunged again, and again I retreated. Some of the men turned to watch, and by the time the play ended with the two mittens in a passionate embrace, everyone was laughing and applauding.

Then we saw Raydon. His mouse's eyes were very bright, and his face was flushed. For some reason, the game with the mittens had made him angry. "What kind of nonsense is this?" he demanded. "Whose are those ridiculous mittens? Aren't the regulation gloves good enough for you?" James reached across and took the mitten from me. All the laughter had gone out of his face. "The mittens are mine," he said. "And far

from being ridiculous, they are the best possible thing for this climate. Regulation gloves! Regulation coats and boots! They may serve to keep a man warm and dry in England, but not in the Arctic. Never." Raydon started to say something about all the years he'd spent in the Navy and all the places he'd visited, but James interrupted him. "Listen, Raydon," he said, his temper flaring. "The Englishman goes to the north in a thin wooden ship with thin wool clothes and thin, dry food. If he is lucky, he comes home after a couple of winters, half dead with cold, maimed with frostbite. If his luck runs out, there is only a pile of stones or a mound in the snow to show where he lies."

He took a long breath, trying to steady himself, before he went on. "The Eskimos have been here for thousands of years, babies and children and old people too. Why are we so stubborn that we will not learn from them?" Raydon fired back, "An Englishman is not an Eskimo! If you think that an English officer would forget his dignity and live like a native, you'd better think again." I laughed. I couldn't help it, the picture in my mind was so vivid: a large Englishman in Navy uniform sitting awkwardly cross-legged, chewing on a hunk of bleeding meat. Raydon glared at me. "There's a thousand years of tradition that tells me he would do no such thing," he finished. "When it is a matter of survival," answered James hotly, "A man does not stand on dignity or on tradition either." "I'll tell you what it takes for survival," said Raydon. "It takes a brave Captain and brave men and discipline. Discipline, I tell you! That's something you don't seem to understand." He was shaking with anger. He tightened his mouth into a thin line. "I must get back to the wheelhouse," he said. Buttoning his coat, a regulation Navy coat with anchors on the buttons, he went up on deck. We all knew that it was not his watch. There was nothing for him to do in the wheelhouse.

Alec cleaned out his pipe and filled it carefully, stuffing the strands of tobacco into the bowl with a stubby finger. The match scraped noisily. He sat in silence, watching the smoke curl and drift. "Regulations!" he said at last. "I've got a bad memory, see. What do the regulations say about eating blubber?" We all laughed and the tension eased a little. Then Dusty said, "You know what I think about at night sometimes? The ice at Banks Land. Forty feet thick, grindin' up on the shore. Even the Eskimos never go there. If Franklin and 'is men are in country like that, God 'elp them. No one else can." "But you're forgetting the things that Doctor Rae brought back to London," said Rob. "They go to prove . . ." "Spoons and buttons and scraps of wood and metal," James interrupted, still angry. "What do they prove?" Before Rob could answer him, there was a cautious cough at the door, and Raydon came in, slapping his hands together. "It's nice and snug in here," he said, looking first at James and then around at the rest of us. James made a place for him at the long table. "Come and sit down. Let's have some water; we'll brew up something hot. Jump to it, boy!" I got up and started for the galley. "There's discipline for you," said James, smiling at Raydon. Then he added seriously, "You are right, of course. Discipline is what it takes to survive—in the Arctic, or anywhere else. Discipline and self-discipline." It can't have been easy for him to say it.

But why was James so very angry? And what is the significance of the spoons and buttons and scraps of wood? What do they have to do with the men of Sir John Franklin's expedition?

July 30

We have been sailing steadily northward up the coast of Greenland. Mr. Hobson says that we are going to make the crossing to the Arctic regions in what they call the North Water. It seemed illogical that we should sail *north* to avoid the ice. He explained, "In the winter the whole of Baffin Bay freezes over. When spring comes, the ice breaks up and drifts south, blocking the passage from east to west. There are three ways to cross. You can sail around the southern edge of the pack. You can take what the whalers call the Middle Passage and push straight through. Or you can go north along the side of the ice until you reach the open water at the top of the Bay, which is what we intend to do. Of course," he said, "there are seasons when none of the three routes is open, but they are few and far between."

Today the carpenter and Davy, his mate, built a

dog pen on deck. It is a serviceable construction, but hardly what a Navy man would call shipshape. I saw Raydon looking at it disapprovingly. Davy finished it off by installing a kennel, an empty ale barrel with one end stove in. Alec and Rob told him that he was wasting his time, the dogs would never use it. "They'll find the windiest, coldest place they can and sleep there," said Rob. Davy ignored him. He folded a ragged old blanket and put it neatly on the floor of the kennel. Davy is shorter than I am. His hair and beard are grizzled brown and cut close. Arranging the blanket, he looked like a little terrier settling itself down for a nap.

August 3

GODHAVN, DISCO ISLAND

Two Eskimos–Samuel Emanuel and Anton Christian –have joined the crew, to serve as dog drivers. Sam (we decided to call him that, it's much easier) has Dick Singleton's bunk, the one below mine. He is very cheerful and smiles a good deal, perhaps because smiling is one of the few ways he has of communicating with us. He doesn't speak any English at all, and we know nothing of the Eskimo language except that one word of James's that means "Good-day," and Sam doesn't seem to understand that. At least, when I said it, he just looked blank.

Sam brought his kayak with him, loaded with fur clothes and what I suppose is hunting gear, though the only thing that looks at all familiar is a harpoon with a beautifully carved bone point. I helped him lash the kayak to the rails, next to one of the ship's boats, and then took him below. Old Harvey told me to see that he was properly fitted out, so I went along to the slop shop and picked out a pair of trousers, a shirt, and a sweater that I thought would fit him. By going through a pantomime of buttoning and unbuttoning, I got him to understand that he was to change out of his clothes and into these. I had forgotten to bring him anything for his feet, so he kept on his long sealskin boots, pulling the legs of the trousers down over them. When he had changed, Rob came over with a pair of scissors and a comb. Sam looked puzzled and even a little scared, so I sat down and let Rob trim my hair first. Sam's was very long, down to his shoulders, and pure black without a hint of red or brown in it. Rob cut it off above his ears and clipped it straight across his forehead in what we used to call a pudding-basin cut. When he had finished, I took Sam up on deck. He walked awkwardly in his new clothes and kept running his hand across the nape of his neck, feeling his stubble-short hair. But he was still smiling.

"You're needed to take the boat ashore," said Raydon, scurrying along the deck after us. "Hurry up now. Nff, nff. He's to go too," he added, pointing at Sam. A boat had been lowered, and the Captain and James were waiting for us. Beside the Captain in the stern sheets sat a big blond man, nearly as tall as Mr. Hobson and broader in the shoulder. The blond man said something to Sam that made him laugh and look down at the furry toes peeping out beneath his trousers. The Captain introduced us. "This is Mr. Petersen. He is Danish, but he was born here and understands the Eskimo language. When we get further north, he will be acting as our interpreter—indeed, he seems to have started work already!" He smiled across at Sam. I had in fact seen the tall Dane come aboard at Godhavn, but had been too busy securing the kayak to pay him much attention. "We are going up the fjord to an Eskimo village," explained the Captain. "Mr. Petersen thinks that we may be able to purchase some dogs there." "Ya, ya," said the interpreter, nodding. I wondered if he could speak English or only Danish and Eskimo. Sam and I will need an interpreter if we are ever to do more than smile at each other. "The fjord is most lovely," Mr. Petersen added and set my doubts to rest.

The fjord was indeed most lovely. The slopes were thick with flowers, yellow, red and bright blue, like pools in the rocks. I saw hares and ptarmigan on the shore, and there were great flocks of ducks on the water, which rose with a flurry when we got near them. But it was a long pull, about three miles, I suppose, and I was glad when Mr. Petersen said at last, "There, on the beach."

It was a big camp, crowded with tents and people, but there were few dogs in sight, and I saw the Captain's face fall. "Tell them that we would like to see all the dogs they have for sale. And say that we will give them a good price," he directed Mr. Petersen. Eleven dogs were paraded in front of us. The Captain looked them over carefully. One he rejected immediately—it had a badly mauled paw—but he bought all the others. The animals seemed half-starved, and the bones of their haunches and shoulders were starkly obvious even through their matted coats. "You pay more for that one," said Mr. Petersen. "Yes, indeed," agreed the Captain, laughing. Even I could see that the dog they were discussing would give birth very soon.

When the negotiations were complete, the Captain asked Mr. Petersen to tell the people to bring the dogs and follow us out to the ship. Sam helped load the dogs into a big skin boat. The villagers looked admiringly at his sweater and trousers; an air of pride replaced the diffidence he had shown when we first got to the camp. I was astonished to see that women took the oars of the boat, though some men climbed in too, to hold the dogs. "That is *umiak,* the woman's boat," explained Mr. Petersen, who must have seen the look on my face. They reached the *Fox* ahead of us.

The bitch appropriated the kennel right away, and I saw Davy look at Rob with a grin that said, "I told you so." Each of the others claimed a few feet of the pen as his own territory. As long as the boundaries were respected, there was peace. But if so much as a claw crossed the invisible line separating one dog's patch from his neighbor's, the hackles rose and the pale eyes glinted. Fortunately there was no actual fighting, perhaps because they are all old acquaintances.

August 4

I didn't join the *Fox* to learn the fishmonger's trade. We took on three barrels of split codfish at Godhavn, and today the Captain set us to work tying the fish to the rigging, so that it will dry and can be stored for the winter. Skewering cold, slippery slabs of fish with a sailmaker's needle and knotting them to the shrouds with wet, slippery twine is not my idea of reasonable work for a sailor. Particularly when there's a howling cold wind blowing.

When I had finished, I went down, reeking of fish, to the boiler room to warm up. James was there, polishing and oiling his precious engine. He wrinkled his nose when I came in, but gave me some warm water and a bar of the special soap he keeps to wash off the engine grease. I sat there for quite a while, enjoying the warmth and the clean, lemony smell of the oil. Twice it was on the tip of my tongue to ask him what he meant about Englishmen being too stubborn to learn from Eskimos, but he was very quiet and I hesitated to break in on his thoughts.

August 5

After supper, Captain McClintock came down to the fo'c'sle. "Good evening, men," he said. "Good evening, sir," we chorused, wondering what he wanted of us.

Perhaps the codfish had slipped the knots and was falling on the deck. "Tomorrow we will be putting in to Upernavik," he said. "It is the last trace of civilization we will meet with for some time, and the last chance to send letters home. I have spare paper and ink, if any of you need it." I followed him up to his cabin. It is no bigger than Mr. Hobson's and impeccably neat. On the shelf above his desk I saw a packet of letters tied with red twill tape and labeled "For the crews of *Erebus* and *Terror*." He followed my glance. "Letters from home," he said. He handed me some paper, enough to write a three-page letter to everyone I have ever met in all my life.

I wrote to Mother. I wanted to tell her that I missed her, and Uncle Dan too, but it is strange how hard it is to put something like that on paper. The sentences were stiff, as if I had taken them direct from a copybook. In the end I filled up the page with facts and figures about the *Fox* and about Greenland that will probably not interest her at all. I sealed the envelope and looked around the fo'c'sle. The men were crowded at the table, elbow to elbow, each in his own private world. Letters for home!

Alec was watching me. When he saw that I had finished my letter, he came across to me. "Would you take something down for me?" he asked. "I'd be glad to," I said, amazed. Alec, the competent, knowledgeable Alec, can't write. I set out a fresh piece of paper and touched up the nib of my pen. He cleared his throat. "Dear Betty," he began and paused. "Well, here we are north again, and in for the long cold. She's a good ship and the Captain and the men are fine fellows too." He stopped, watching my hand. "... fine fellows too," I wrote. "Ready," I said. He thought for a moment, chewing his lower lip. "Look after yourself, Betty, until I'm back. Your loving husband." I gave him the pen and he wrote a careful "Alexander."

August 6
UPERNAVIK

The wind has gone round three points, and all day storm clouds have been building up in the north. Because of the weather, we didn't stay long in Upernavik, just long enough to land the letters and take on board eighteen more sled dogs.

We had expected trouble with the dogs, and trouble we got. The fighting began when the first of the newcomers was put in the pen. In no time, all of them were at each others' throats; even the bitch came out of the kennel and joined in. Sam pulled his long driving whip out of his belt and vaulted over the railing. He seized the two dogs nearest him by the scruff of the neck, pulled them apart, and heaved them to opposite sides of the pen. Punching, kicking, and whipping, he separated the others. One big gray creature, which had been in the very middle of the fight, got a blow behind the ear and fell unconscious on the deck. I had never seen dogs, even the most vicious, treated like that. "It is the only way with sled dogs," said Mr. Petersen, standing beside me. "You teach them from the beginning who is master." The gray dog came to and stood shakily in the center of the pen, challenging the others to renew the fighting. Sam lashed at him with the whip until the animal whimpered and lay down. Mr. Petersen said, "You do not make a—how do you say?—a pet of a sled dog. You wish that he serves you, not that he likes you." He laughed. "Friend of mine, he hits his dogs on the heads with a hammer. His dogs are the most good dogs in the town."

August 7

The storm that threatened yesterday caught us in the early hours with gale-force winds, rain and heavy seas. We are hove-to with only the topsails set, and it looks as if even they will be blown out of the bolt-ropes. Alec keeps glancing up anxiously; if the canvas rips, he's the one who will have to mend it.

There is water everywhere. It comes in green over the weather rail and washes across the deck thigh-deep. It spills down the companionway and drips through the skylight above my bunk. It slops back and forth on the fo'c'sle floor, trundling slippers and mess-kits and all kinds of oddments with it. It dribbles down necks and up sleeves. To be soaked through when you have laboriously tied soul-and-body lashings around your wrists and waist and ankles is too much for anyone's temper. Alec says, "It's best to get wet and stay wet." He's a lot hardier than I am.

With each wave the dogs are swept off their feet and across the pen into a yelping heap against the far rail. They sort themselves out, shake themselves off, and then the water comes at them again. Sharing this misery, they've forgotten about the boundary lines. In all the ship only the fawn bitch has been warm and dry all day. Sam brought her below when the storm started and put her on his bunk. She curled up there, looking very smug.

August 9

Five puppies were born during the night. They are ugly little things, almost hairless, with square, wrinkled faces, but Sam seems as pleased as if they were his own children.

One of the puppies was much smaller than the others. It lay by itself on the edge of the bunk, while its brothers and sisters burrowed energetically at their mother's side. Sam pushed two of the larger puppies away and gently put the little runt in their place. It sucked weakly for a minute or two, then lost its hold on the teat and fell back. Sam pointed at it, hung his head limply, and closed his eyes. He meant that the puppy would die. I picked up the tiny thing. Its bones were sharp under its silky skin, and its heart beat against my fingers like the tick of a watch that is running down. I tucked it carefully inside my jacket and went to the galley. "There ain't much 'ope for 'im, far as I can tell," said Cooky, "but there's no 'arm in tryin'." He made a paste of flour and warm water and sugar. I dipped my finger in the mixture and held it to the puppy's mouth, easing it under his soft lips. He licked at it feebly.

When I got back, the bitch and the puppies were gone, and Sam was straightening his bedding. "Where are the dogs?" I asked. Of course he didn't understand; I keep forgetting. Alec answered, "The Captain says no dogs below decks. He's right, too. I mean it. They won't thrive if they stay down here in the warm." I hid the little runt in a fold of my blanket; he will never survive in competition with his brothers and sisters.

August 10

I have named the puppy Pip. "Would that be short for pip-squeak?" asked Raydon unpleasantly and said that he'd tell the Captain. I don't think that he will, though.

The others are sympathetic about my keeping the puppy below decks—except for Old Harvey, who pretends that he doesn't notice.

Every two hours or so last night, I fed Pip with the flour and water mixture, pushing it into his mouth until he closed his lips against my finger and refused to take any more. This morning he seemed a little stronger, but Sam looked at him and again did his mimicry of death. Pip is cold now, but I daren't put him in my bunk, in case I should roll over in my sleep and suffocate him.

August 11

I woke early for the forenoon watch, just as seven bells struck, but I'd slept too long. Pip was dead, stiff and cold. In death, he seemed terribly small. He fitted easily into my cupped hands. There was still a scum of the flour and water paste around his mouth from the last feeding. Poor tiny thing.

I wrapped him in a piece of oiled silk. Somehow I didn't want him to float, but I couldn't think of anything to use as a weight. There was nothing suitable in the carpenter's shop. In the boiler room I found some spare bolts that would have served the purpose well, but I thought James might miss them. In the end I went to the galley. It was full of steam; Cooky was boiling up oatmeal for breakfast. He saw me come in and scooped a little of the gruel onto a plate. "Somethin' for the puppy," he called. "He's dead. It's too late," I said, trying to ignore the lump in my throat. "I wondered if there was anything I could use to . . . something I could have so that he will sink." "That's a shame," said Cooky. "Somethin' to bury 'im in, you wanted. Well, let's see." He reached to the back of a shelf and handed me a box that had held five pounds of tea. "You could pound some 'oles in that," he suggested. "It would go down."

The box bobbed brightly on the water for a couple of minutes and then sank. I turned away and looked across at the kennel. The other puppies are twice as big as Pip was. Perhaps Sam was right and he never had a chance.

August 13

Today the water was like glass, scratched over with the crisscross wakes of thousands and thousands of eider ducks. We steamed on north, with the sails hanging in heavy swags from the yards. By evening the codfish in the rigging was smelling very strong.

August 15

We are now well up into Baffin Bay, and there is still no sign of the North Water. The Captain was aloft in the crow's nest for the better part of the morning, looking to the north and west through a powerful telescope.

James is teaching Sam a little English; Sam, in return, is adding to James's one-word Eskimo vocabulary. (Anton doesn't seem to want to learn. He keeps himself busy with the dogs, as silent as the Smiths.) I was cutting down the rotted codfish from the rigging—the Captain has finally decided that his experiment has failed—and heard some of the lesson. They were looking across the water to the pack ice, which is close on the port side. "Ice," said James, pointing. He said the word very slowly and distinctly, a sigh and a hiss. "Eye-uss," said Sam, exaggerating. Then he pointed in his turn. *"Sikuliak,"* he said. *"Pogazak."* He waved his hand toward the horizon. *"Pakaliak."* James tried the words, getting a little tangled. I slithered down the rigging. "What was he saying?" I asked. "He was telling me the words for 'ice,' " answered James. "Three words?" I was doubtful. "Listen," said James. "A city man sees the country as just one stretch of green. The farmer knows that this is pasture and that is young oats, or hay, or whatever it may be. We're strangers here; we look at the pack and see only ice. But the Eskimos know that this is young ice and that is old ice; this is safe to walk on, that is full of holes. Of course they have more than one word. They probably have more than the three he told me." "Eye-uss, *pogazak,*" said Sam, leaning over the rail. Close to the *Fox* the ice was soft and broken, as if it had been through a giant coffee-mill. *"Pogazak,"* I said confidently, and Sam grinned at me.

August 16

This morning the Captain went aloft again. When he came down, his face was bleak. "Change course. Steer southwest," he said briefly to Rob, who was at the wheel. "Aye, aye, sir," said Rob, startled. So we've given up hope of making the crossing in the North Water. It's a dead end.

Rob headed the *Fox* up into the wind and swung her around. The booms came across slowly, creaking. The ship, having come so far, seemed reluctant to turn back. We began beating to the southwest, close to the edge of the ice, searching for an opening that might let us through. There was no sign of life, except for a few straggling birds. Sam, looking astern, said "Snow sky." His English is progressing far faster than my Eskimo.

August 18

We beat along for two dreary days and nights, with the snow sky dark behind us. But today, toward evening, the wind went round abruptly and started to blow hard from the south. Almost at once the ice began to shift and lanes of open water appeared in the pack. The Captain gave Mr. Hobson the telescope. "Your eyes are younger than mine," he said. "You choose the lead." His voice was controlled, as always, but Mr. Hobson's "Yes, *sir,*" almost squeaked with excitement. He scrambled up to the crow's nest, nearly losing his footing in his haste. After a while he straightened his back, pulling himself up to his full six-and-a-half feet, and pointed due west. "Clear to the horizon! This is the one!" he shouted down. We turned into the lead. It was perhaps a mile across, dark between its margins of ice. Alec cupped his hands. "Can you hear me, America-a-a?" he called. Everyone laughed. We're a long way off yet, but the lead is open as far as the eye can see, stretching across the bay to the Arctic regions.

September 4

We must have been a quarter of the way across when the wind, which had opened the ice to let us in, clamped it shut around us and cut off both advance and retreat. Captain McClintock ordered the rudder and propellor unshipped. It seemed to me a humiliating surrender to the pack, and I said as much to James. "The ice can twist iron as easily as you can bend a green ash twig," he said. "You don't believe me now, but you will before the winter is out."

The pack is drifting slowly to the northwest, taking us with it. At least we have the comfort of going in the right direction, even if a rudderless drift isn't the method we would have chosen—if we'd had the choice. Mr. Hobson says that other ships have been trapped like this and have broken free in time to go into winter quarters on the American Arctic shore.

The ice is always in motion—you can hear it, even when you can't see it. Sometimes it presses so hard on the ship that the timbers groan; other times it pulls back and leaves us clear. Whenever a sizable crack opens up ahead, there is a shout: "All hands to the track-rope!" We struggle into our tracking belts—"row-daddies," the old hands call them, I don't know why—and jump down onto the ice. The heavy track-rope, coiled ready on the deck, is flung over the side. We drag it ahead of the ship and, like a team of barge horses, pull her through the ice. The rope cuts into our hands and shoulders until our muscles and even our bones shriek with the strain. Sweat pours from our heads and chests and backs, but we are up to our knees in icy slush and our feet are numb. "Away, haul away, rock and roll me over. Away, haul away, haul away—*pull!*" Finally the order, "Alright, men, slack off now." We drop the rope and look behind us. The *Fox* has advanced maybe ten feet from her old position.

No, I should be fair. On at least two occasions we hauled her several hundred feet through the ice, and once we made nearly two miles. That time, after sliding her through a succession of small pools, we were checked by a hummock of ice. A two-pound explosive charge was brought from the munitions store and we backed the *Fox* away. James bored a deep hole in the hummock, slipped in the explosive and packed snow firmly over it. He laid the fuse across the ice and then stood by while Mr. Brands struck the match. The chief engineer is in charge of explosions, apparently. The flame fizzed slowly along and died in a patch of wet snow. James relit it and ran back with his hands over his ears. He ran clumsily, like someone who is out of the habit of it. When I think back, I don't remember ever having seen him move faster than a very deliberate walk. There was a dull thud, which seemed to come from right under my feet, and the hummock burst open, scattering blackened ice in every direction. We went up to the hole. The hummock had gone, but in its place was a worse obstacle, a thick soup of broken ice welling up from below.

Rob has been reading Hakluyt's *Voyages,* a battered copy from the seamen's library. "I didn't know you were a scholar," I said. "I'm not really. Not like James. There's no end to the things he knows. But there's something about these old sailors. . . ." He riffled through the book. "Setting out on a voyage and never knowing what they'd find. Mermaids or monsters or the edge of the world. Or the Orient—silks and ivories and spices, waiting at the end of the Northwest Passage, if they could only find it." "Frobisher and Hudson," I said, remembering history lessons. "Right, and others after them, all looking for a sea route to the Orient." "And none of them succeeding," I said flatly. "None of them succeeding," he agreed, "but each of them getting a little farther and finding out a little more. So that by the time Franklin sailed, it was all laid out on the map, the whole of the Northwest Passage from one end to the other, all but one stretch. Like a puzzle with one piece missing."

September 10

To the west there are five or six large icebergs. If they are aground, as the Captain suspects, it would explain the fact that the westward drift of the pack has slowed almost to a standstill. (If the pack stops moving, of course, we do too. And if we don't move, westward and soon, we'll be prisoners in the ice the whole winter.) So yesterday Mr. Hobson and I set out across the pack to find out.

We took a little food and some measuring instruments on the small sled. I put on my high boots and was glad that I did: almost first thing, I misjudged the width of a puddle and splashed right in. Wet feet are no joke in this latitude. After that, I watched every step. The newly formed ice was almost black, saturated with water, and very unsafe. *Sikuliak? Pakaliak?* I don't remember. We stayed on the old ice, walking carefully and far apart. We saw a family of seals sunning themselves on the ice, the big bull lifting his head from time to time, alert for danger. Mr. Hobson stopped and loaded his gun, but before he could fire the seals slipped off the ice into a pool of open water. "They keep better watch than we do," he called back, laughing. I wondered if he was thinking of the day that my stint in the crow's nest cost us three planks. If he was, I couldn't see it in his face, at least not at that distance. A little farther on we found the tracks of a polar bear, each print as wide as my two hands put together. Probably the bear had been watching the seals and us too. Perhaps he was still watching us.

After about four hours' hard walking, we reached the nearest of the icebergs. It rose up sheer, three mainmasts high, broad as a meadow. Its eastern side, facing the drifting pack, was piled with broken ice to a height of fifty feet or more. The *Fox* would shatter on this cliff like an egg thrown against a wall.

The matches were wet, and there was a gusty wind blowing. With considerably difficulty we lit the stove, melted some snow, and made a pot of lukewarm tea to wash down the hunks of bread and pemmican. Mr. Hobson took a bite and grimaced. "The label says, 'Manufactured only from prime beef and best-quality suet,' " he complained. "This tastes as if they had used broken-down horses and old candle ends." It tasted alright to me, though it did need a lot of chewing.

When we had finished our uncomfortable meal, Mr. Hobson set up the theodolite to measure the height of the iceberg, and I started boring through the ice to get a sounding. We compared our findings. Height, 250 feet. Sea bottom at 83 fathoms. So the iceberg is aground, except perhaps at spring tides, and the others are probably grounded too.

The measurements had taken more time than we had thought; the sun was almost down when we started back for the *Fox*. In the oblique light, the going was even harder. Mr. Hobson stumbled waist-deep in a snowdrift, lost his balance and dropped his gun. We dug into the drift like a pair of terriers at a rathole, but the gun was nowhere to be found. I remembered the huge tracks of the polar bear. He would be hungry now and hunting his dinner. Sleet began to fall, and the rising wind blew it in our faces. My feet became completely numb and my hands stiffened, clawlike, around the sled rope. I trudged on and on, with my head lowered and my eyes almost shut, following Mr. Hobson's footprints. On and on, feeling nothing except the cold, thinking only of the next step and the next. Suddenly, quite close, there was a discordant outburst of barking—one of the most welcome sounds I ever heard.

Extra lights were burning in the wheelhouse. There were white patches on Mr. Hobson's cheeks and his moustache was crusted with ice. He nodded at me and his eyes smiled. I tried to smile back and was surprised to find that I couldn't move my lips. The doctor came up on deck, shrugging his coat on over his nightshirt.

I saw concern and then alarm in his face. He hustled Mr. Hobson off to his cabin. Someone took me by the elbows and all but carried me to the fo'c'sle. Sam was still awake, or maybe the dogs' barking had awakened him. He pulled off my boots and gloves and wrapped my feet in his blanket. He unbuttoned my jacket and my shirt and made me put my hands on my bare stomach. There was no feeling in my fingers. Signaling with the flat of his hand, as you do to a dog when you want him to sit, he went away. When he came back, it was with a cold, wet rag, which he held against my cheeks and chin. The doctor came in and watched him for a while. "He knows what to do better than I," he said to me. "You'll be alright now. Sleep as long as you want. No work for you tomorrow." When I fell asleep, the blood was still burning in my fingers and toes.

I slept right through until dinnertime, waking to the mouth-watering smell of boiled pork and onions. I hadn't eaten since the pemmican picnic at the iceberg. Cooky gave me twice my share, and the hollowness in my stomach disappeared. After dinner I added two more marks to the lengthening line on the post by my bunk. Usually I don't have time to make more than a quick cut, just to record the day, but with nothing else to do I concentrated on the carving. The mark for yesterday wasn't very successful. I wanted to carve a seal, but there was a knot in the wood just where the flippers should have gone, so I turned it into a dog whip with an outsize handle. Today's mark is much better, a *J* with swirls and curlicues that a lawyer's clerk might be proud of. I had no trouble holding the knife, but I noticed raw-looking red spots on my hands. My feet were the same, and swollen too, as I found when I tried to put my boots on. I shuffled up on deck in a pair of canvas slippers.

The sun was warm, though there was a brisk wind. James was sitting in the lee of the wheelhouse, darning his socks. I slid down beside him. "I heard that you and Mr. Hobson were in bad shape when you got back last night," he said. He looked me up and down, frowning when he saw the slippers. "Are your feet sore?" "Yes, a little, and my hands too." "Let me see." I pulled my hands out of my pockets. They looked worse in the sunlight, mottled and lumpy. James tut-tutted to himself. "You must keep an eye on those fingers," he said. "Frostbite is a dangerous thing. If it is neglected, it can kill a man." He sat silent for a moment, his eyes focused on something very distant—the past, perhaps. Then he gave himself a little shake and went on, "I thought you would be worse, though. Davy said he could hardly get you down the hatchway, you were so stiff." So it was Davy who had carried me down. He's stronger than I'd thought. "Sam put cold water on my face, where it was frozen," I said. "Why did he do that? I'd have thought it would be better to use something hot." "Sam did exactly the right thing, you can be sure of that." "After all, his people have lived here for generations," I finished, remembering the argument that had started with the mittens and James's anger at Raydon.

I knew that he was remembering it too, because he drew down his brows sharply. My curiosity got the better of me. "What did Raydon say that night to make you so angry?" "It wasn't Raydon, really. It was the whole stubborn, tradition-bound system that has made Raydon what he is. It was unfair of me to attack him; he's not to blame for the Sea Lords' stupidities." "Stupidities?" I was shocked by the word. The Sea Lords had always been like gods to me, all-wise and all-powerful. "What do you mean?"

James didn't answer immediately. He bit off a new piece of yarn, threaded his needle—at the first try—and stretched a sock smoothly over the darning egg. "It's a strong word, I grant you, but I don't think it's too strong, when you consider what happened. You've heard of Sir John Ross?" "No, I'm afraid I haven't." "They called him the Grand Old Man of the Arctic. This was before Franklin's time, you understand. Well, Ross took an expedition north to the Magnetic Pole. From the very beginning, everything went wrong. It's a long story, but to cut it short, the ship was frozen in and they had to desert her out there in the middle of nowhere. If it hadn't been for the Eskimos, they would all have died. The Eskimos showed them how to travel, how to hunt and live off the land, what to do when they got frostbite and snow blindness—and all but three got home safely. And what did the Sea Lords do? They completely ignored everything Ross and his men had learned. They went on doing things the way they had always been done. They had nothing to learn from the natives, they said; they knew it all already. But every time they sent an expedition to the Arctic, men died by the score."

His tone was very dry, as if he had aloes on his tongue. I wondered if someone he had known had been among those who died. "My father was with Ross's expedition, you see. That's why I feel so strongly about it. No, he wasn't one of the three who died, but he came back with stumps instead of fingers on his right hand. It was frostbite. He'd got it before they learned the right way to manage it, and the surgeon had had to amputate. He used to feel an excruciating pain in his fingers—the fingers he'd left in the Arctic. Strange."

"What about Sir John Franklin and his men?" I asked. "What do you think has happened to them?" "If they had the chance and the sense to learn from the Eskimos, they could still be alive," he said. "Twelve years is a long time, I agree, but as you said yourself, people have been living here for generations and generations." James gathered up his mending and tied his sewing kit with a spare length of yarn. "Don't worry," he added. "We're going to be alright. Captain McClintock is a different breed of man. He knows how to live with the cold almost as well as an Eskimo. And anyway, he's not a stubborn Englishman—he's Irish!"

September 13

A cold, overcast day. Over us, and behind us to the east, the clouds are white, reflecting the snow-covered pack. But to the west, about fifteen miles off, they are dark. There is water there. You can see in the sky almost exactly where the ice ends and the open sea begins. Fifteen miles away . . . but we have no means of getting there. The Captain hasn't said anything, but it's clear to all of us that we're stuck here for the winter. And that means yet another season in the Arctic for Franklin's men.

September 20

I'm teaching Sam to play checkers. He's picking up the game very fast, and if I don't watch out he'll soon be beating me. Every time we play, Raydon comes by. "Nff, nff." Obviously he disapproves. But does he disapprove of checkers, or does he disapprove of *Sam* playing checkers? Is he thinking, "The Eskimo boy should be kept in his place"? If he is, he'd better keep his thought to himself.

September 28

Sam went seal-hunting today and took me with him. He brought a coil of leather thongs, a knife, several strange-looking tools whose purpose I couldn't guess at, and his harpoon, the one with the carved bone point. As well as all this, he carried his kayak, balanced on his head. I took nothing except our dinner, pemmican sandwiches again. I offered to help him with some of the load, but he pointed at my feet, shook his head, and laughed. He meant, I think, that I should concentrate on keeping my footing. And, in fact, it was all I could do to keep up with him.

We went east over the pack. It was very slow going. In places the ice was rafted up into piles twenty or thirty feet high, and we had to climb. In other places there were puddles or cracks or stretches of the dark, waterlogged young ice. All of these we avoided if we could, even if it meant going a long way round. For every mile of forward progress, we must have zigzagged at least three.

After two hours or so, we found open water, lying like a lake in the ice-field. Several seals looked at us curiously with large round eyes, and then dived down. I started walking on tip-toe and made an effort to breathe quietly, but at the same moment Sam, who must have seen the seals too, began to stamp and whistle and wave his arms around. I was surprised; he seemed to be deliberately drawing attention to himself. One of the seals surfaced briefly, closer this time, and watched him. It was obviously intrigued by what he was doing.

Still whistling and stamping, Sam took off his mittens and fetched the bundle of thongs. He knotted them together so that they formed a long line, and tied

one end to his harpoon. Then he took up position on the very edge of the ice, whistling, waiting, with his elbow bent and the slender harpoon angled upward. A seal's head broke the surface and the harpoon flashed over the water, with the line flicking behind it. The creature went down in a long struggling dive. Sam ran back from the water, pulling in the thong hand over hand. The seal came up threshing in a froth of blood and blubber, and he hauled it onto the ice and clubbed it on the head.

After that, I didn't feel like eating lunch, though it was getting late. We started back, Sam with the kayak and me dragging the seal by a length of thong tied around its back flippers. About half a mile from home we almost fell into a lane of open water. There had been solid ice there when we left. We crossed on the kayak, two of us on a one-man boat. Sam sat across the stern and I straddled the bow, feeling very precarious. The seal floated along behind.

The dogs smelled the fresh meat and came tearing out across the ice. Sam managed to keep them off and we got his prize on board intact. He set to work to cut it up. The Captain came on deck and watched him admiringly—he certainly is very quick and neat with his knife. Cooky brought a tray and took the liver, as well as several large chunks of meat from the seal's sides. The rest of it Sam put on the meat rack out on the ice. The dogs clamored round, but the rack had been carefully built to be out of their reach.

There was seal steak for supper tonight, and Sam was lord of the feast. James proposed a toast: "To Sam, a most excellent hunter, the provider of this evening's meal and more meals to come." Sam didn't understand all the words, but he knew that they were praising him and beamed. I couldn't eat the meat and made myself a cracker hash instead. It was a good hash, the biscuit pounded well with water and plenty of strawberry jam. Cooky took it out of the oven at exactly the right time, so that it was neither soggily under-done nor over-cooked and caramelized. I don't know why I balked at eating the seal. Perhaps if I had killed it myself it might have been different. I've shot rabbits and eaten them often enough—and enjoyed it, too.

October 4

Getting the *Fox* snugged in for the winter took days of hard work. First the topmasts and the yards were sent down. Then we hauled the heavy canvas housing into place, so that it covered the deck from the foremast to the mizzen like a gigantic tent. The peak was lashed to the booms, and the sides were stretched over the rails to keep the wind out. With the housing secured, we built a bank of snow around the whole ship, as high as the gunwales and wide enough at the top for two men to walk abreast. We carved out a series of burrows for the dogs—in the moonlight they look like a row of monstrous black buttons—and built a stairway amidships. Last of all, we packed snow in solidly on the decks and over the sky-lights. Now only a gray light comes into the fo'c'sle, and only for a few hours at midday.

October 13

I tried to persuade one of the puppies to walk with me, but it was happy in its snow hole and refused to budge. So I walked by myself. It was unbelievably lonely out on the pack. Nothing but ice and snow and sky. No color. No movement. Not a sign of a living thing, not even a solitary bird.

Coming in out of the cold, the fo'c'sle seemed like a washhouse on Monday morning, hot and damp and close. And noisy! Alec was picking out a hymn tune on the organ, while Sam turned the handle. Davy was following him on his flute, usually a beat and a half behind. Jackson, Cooky, Dusty, and Old Harvey were playing cards, with a lot of shouting and laughing and slapping down of chips on the table. Rob and James were talking–about me, I think, because when they saw me coming they stopped abruptly.

Alec limped to the end of "Rock of Ages" and came over and joined us. "I always had a fancy to sit up there in the organ loft," he said. "But the more I practice, the worse I get. Oh well . . . Where've you been?

Out walking?" he asked me. "Yes," I said, "It's beastly cold." "You'll get used to it. Why, I remember going out all day, up in Mercy Bay, hunting hares, see, and coming back warmer that when I left. I mean it. And that was a sight nearer the Pole." "There are hares that far north?" "Oh yes. White ones. Very wild and fierce, they are. There was one day I sighted a hare, around noontime it was, and shot off three of his legs. He ran and I ran after him, see, until it was dark and I had to let him go. Then there was Tom's hare. He was my mate, see. He shot the fur off one side of it, but it got away. It's still traveling around up there, half naked." I stared at him. His face was perfectly straight. "Are you pulling my leg?" I asked. Rob and James put their heads down on the table and laughed until they could hardly get their breath. When will I ever learn?

October 27

For the past week we have been working with the sleds, men and dogs alike. The Captain laid out a course across some five miles of ice, and this is where we pull the sleds. Out past the scrap pits to Harmsworth's Hollow (named for Rob, who got himself thoroughly stuck in a snowdrift there), and then back through the Cut. The Cut is a long stretch of level ice, with high ice walls on both sides. Our team—Rob and Davy and

Dusty and I—always goes through the Cut at a gallop. It's the only part of the course where you can be really sure of your footing, and besides, it's the homestretch.

The Captain is always there for sled practice. He loads the sleds himself, with twenty-pound tins of pemmican, and writes down the total weight for each sled. He also notes the time it takes each team to cover the five-mile course. We discovered today the purpose of all this note-taking: he is trying to find out exactly how much weight a man can pull, and how far he can pull it before he gets tired. We also discovered that our team, with its gallop through the Cut, had been upsetting all his calculations. He was very nice about it, though, and only said, "It never occurred to me that you would want to *run* with a loaded sled."

Yesterday I spent with the dogs, helping Sam. I had supposed that they were trained sled-dogs. If they were, they had forgotten everything they ever knew. We got harnesses onto seven of them without too much difficulty and led them out across the ice to the sled. That was where the trouble started. Perhaps they did remember one thing from their training: a sled meant work. They wouldn't sit still long enough for us to attach the traces. In the end I held each one between my knees while Sam did up the buckles. Then he sent the whip cracking and snaking over their backs, and they started off—each at a different speed and each in a different direction. In no time at all, the traces were in a hopeless tangle. Using our teeth and our bare hands, we unknotted them and began again. The same thing happened. Left to myself, I would probably have gone back and abandoned the dogs to tie themselves up to their hearts' content, but Sam was endlessly patient. Start and tangle and stop; untangle and start again. Over and over. I had thought that dog-sledding would be a grand, swift ride, a snowy steeplechase. It's far less trouble and far less tiring to pull the sled yourself.

October 30

I still don't like Raydon one bit, but I have to hand it to him: he is a real musician. This evening he took a flute out of his sea chest and began to play, sitting in the shadows behind the stove. The sound was very soft, but clear and true. Compared to this, Davy's flute is like a cracked penny whistle. The tunes he played were the old ones, "Barb'ra Allen" and "Lord Randal" and "The Ash Grove," country songs with long phrases curling back on themselves. I knew them all, but when he played them it was like hearing them for the first time. "That was beautiful, Raydon. I mean it," said Alec. "Yes indeed," said Rob. "Takes me back to when I was a boy." Raydon didn't answer them, but I could see that he was pleased.

There were traces of tears in James's eyes. " 'Lord Randal' was Grace's favorite song," he said. "My wife's. I can never hear it now without thinking of her." "I didn't know that you were married," I said, surprised.

James had never joined in the toast to wives and sweethearts or talked at all about his home. "I don't look like a married man, do I? No. I was a married man for almost a year." He had been teaching in a village school then—so I *was* right—and she had waited for him every afternoon at the schoolyard gate. The sun had slanted down on her through the leaves, dusty yellow fall leaves. "And then she died, giving birth to a stillborn girl. I went away, as far as I could, to the sea."

November 1

The sun has gone. We won't see it again this year, or well into next year, for that matter.

The doctor has started a school. There are classes in reading, writing, and arithmetic. They use all the lamps in the fo'c'sle. Alec hasn't joined the classes; he says he's too old to learn.

November 4

Sam beat me at checkers tonight, for the first time. But we'll have to make some more pieces before we play again. When Mr. Hobson shouted down the hatchway, we jumped up in such a hurry that the board fell over and the checkers rolled away under the corner bunks. "A bear on the ice, fighting with the dogs!"

As I came on deck a rifle fired, very close. The flash was a cruel, brilliant orange in the dark. The bullet must have hit, I think, because there was a furious roar, but it was hard to see. The bear was only an indistinct shape against the snow, the center of a circle of yelping dogs. The circle swayed and broke and closed again. A dog howled in pain. Shadowy figures went cautiously out over the ice—the officers, each with his rifle at the ready. There was another flash, and it was all over.

The bear was a big one, over seven feet long. The Captain will give the skin to Lady Franklin. It will lie on a hearth somewhere in England, staring at the fire with green glass eyes. How far away it seems—home, I mean.

The bear's head was very small, compared with its huge body. There didn't seem much room for brain between the little eyes. "Are they intelligent, polar bears?" I asked Old Harvey, remembering that he had hunted them at least once before, with Abbott. "Oh, they're cunning enough," he said. "Mind you, I've never seen this, but I've been told it's true. When they go hunting, they carry a piece of ice in front of them." "What ever for?" "Can't you think that out for yourself?" he asked, sitting back and twiddling his thumbs. It's a trick he has; he says it keeps his hands from getting as stiff as his knees. "No, I . . . Oh! Their noses are black. They'd be very conspicuous. They're trying to hide their noses?" "That's right," he said, "But like I said, I've never seen them do it. One thing they do, though, when they want to catch a seal by surprise. They push themselves along by their back legs, with their front legs doubled up under them. That's why there's no fur on their paws; they rub them bare." "That's ridiculous!" I said. "Go up and look for yourself, then," he answered. Sure enough, the front paws were hairless.

I went to James with this piece of information, because I thought he would be interested. He refused to believe it. "But I saw his paws myself," I protested. "You didn't see him crawling on them, did you?" His tone was patronizing and I lost my temper. "You always have to be right, don't you?" I said furiously. "You think you know everything. But you don't. You may have been a schoolmaster once, but you're not any more. You're just an ordinary sailor, like the rest of us. You may be older than I am, but that doesn't give you the right to patronize me or to be sarcastic, either. I tell you, James, I won't stand for it." I really was angry. I still am.

November 6

Sam invited the Captain to go for a sled ride tomorrow at midday, when the light is best. He accepted. "Thank you. I shall look forward to it." Sam invited me as well. Remembering the last time I was out with the dogs, I'm not sure I look forward to it at all.

James hasn't said an unnecessary word to me for three days, and I haven't spoken to him. He's waiting for me to apologize. I know that I shouldn't have yelled at him like that, but I still think I was right. He didn't have to be so beastly patronizing. It is very awkward, though, not speaking to someone when you are practically living in his lap.

November 7

I can hardly believe that these are the same dogs as the ones I had wanted to abandon as being hopeless. Part of the difference is that they now have a leader. She is slate gray, smaller than the others and very bright. With Sophie harnessed in the middle position, the team works as a team.

The Captain stood on the back of the sled, holding on to the supports. The whip cracked, the dogs leaned into their harnesses, and off we went—straight ahead! The sled bounced and swayed but the Captain held on. Even though the lower part of his face was wrapped round with an old checked muffler, I could tell that he was laughing. We got up a bit of speed. I was timing my steps, getting ready to jump onto the sled, when it stopped with a jerk that pitched him off into the snow. It had rammed a hummock, so hard that the runners had sliced in and stuck. The dogs were on the far side of the mound, lying in the snow with their tongues lolling out. They all looked extremely pleased with themselves, as if the whole purpose of the expedition had been to bury the sled and make a snowman of the Captain. After that, though, as if to make amends, they behaved beautifully: they only got tangled once in the two hours that we were out.

Three of the dogs, including Sophie, look very shabby. Their winter coats haven't grown in yet, though, goodness knows, it's cold enough. When we got back, the Captain said to Sam, "Bring these three on deck. Give them a good meal." He spoke slowly, pointing first at the dogs and then at the ship, to make sure that Sam got his meaning. He doesn't know that Sam understands almost everything we say, though he speaks very little himself. So tonight Sophie and the other two gorged themselves in the shelter of the housing, while the others scrabbled for their dinner as usual, out on the ice.

November 9

It was a mistake to feed those three dogs on deck. Tonight the whole pack, with Sophie in the lead, charged the ship. I was in the wheelhouse, fiddling with the lamp, trying to adjust it so that it would burn without smoking, and didn't see them until they were nearly on top of me. They swept around my legs and off under the housing. I yelled, "The dogs are on board!" and started after them. The men came bursting up the hatchway, Rob in his nightshirt and slippers, Alec in a red-and-white-striped stocking cap, Davy fighting into a sweater, Sam and Anton fully dressed in furry layers. But not James. We chased the dogs around the deck, trying to corner them, but they were old hands at that game and dodged and feinted and hid in out-of-the-way corners all over the ship. It was a good hour before we drove them all back down onto the ice. We built a makeshift barrier to keep them out and retreated below to count our losses. A broomstick and a coil of rope had been captured by the invaders, a shirt had been torn, Alec had lost his cap, and Rob was missing a slipper. He had aimed a kick at one of the dogs, the slipper had flown off his foot, and the "miserable brute," as he called him, had carried it away in triumph. "And I hope it gives him indigestion," he added.

November 12

James fell down the hatchway yesterday morning. Slipped on the ice at the top, I think. It's easy enough to slip there. I didn't see the fall, but I heard it and knew it was bad. We found him lying half on the ladder, half on the floor. His head was twisted into his shoulder. "Don't move him," said Alec. "Get the doctor." Davy went, I think. There wasn't a stretcher, of course, so they slid a piece of canvas under him and moved him to the nearest bunk.

How long ago was that? Twelve hours? More? He hasn't moved or made a sound in all that time. They put a plaid blanket over him. If you watch carefully, you can see the blue and green lines shift with his breathing. That's the only sign that he is still alive. His face is pale, and the furrows from his nose to the corners of his mouth make deep shadows. There is engine grease under his fingernails.

Everyone is very quiet. They come in soft-footed and bend over him, watching. But Sam won't look at him at all. He is involved in some silent ceremony of his own. He has changed his clothes and covered his face with a cloth.

I asked the doctor if there was a chance. "It's touch and go. That's all I can tell you. Touch and go."

November 13

No change. Perhaps this is the deep healing sleep that women talk about. "Let him have his sleep out. He'll be the better for it." "Two days' sleep for each day's fever." But James has no fever.

November 14

James is dead, and the funeral is tomorrow. He never regained consciousness, just breathed slower and slower until he stopped breathing altogether. I couldn't tell which was the last breath.

Jackson measured him for a coffin. Alec went through his things and found a fresh white shirt to bury him in. Davy and Raydon and Rob practiced a hymn for the service tomorrow. I wish there was something *I* could do, but everything that can be done has been done, I suppose. All there is for me is to sit and remember. He wasn't patronizing or sarcastic or any of the other things I said. I can't take the words back now. Or ever.

November 15

We went out in the noon twilight to cut a hole in the ice for James's grave and to put direction posts in the snow so that we could find our way there in the dark. The ice was nearly four feet thick. I have been back to the place several times since, with a pole, to stir the water and prevent it from freezing over. Now there is nothing to do except wait.

Later

They carried the coffin up on deck and covered it with a flag. Captain McClintock read the burial service there, his voice very low and his hands shaking a little, holding the prayer book. "Unto almighty God we commend the soul of our brother departed, and we commit his body to the deep; earth to earth, dust to dust, in sure and certain hope of the resurrection to eternal life. . . ." The dogs were howling out on the ice, and I lost the next words. ". . . the earth and the sea shall give up their dead. . . ." Drowned men in a procession stretching back to the beginning of time, the Orkney men who went down in sight of their homes, sailors buried at sea, and James the last of them all. We put the coffin on a sled and pulled it out to the hole in the ice. The *Fox*'s colors were at half-mast and the bell was tolling. It was still and intensely cold. The Captain repeated, "We commit his body to the deep," and the coffin slid down into the black water.

Mr. Hobson walked beside me on the way back to the ship. "He thought a lot of you, you know. He told me you had the makings of a real sailor, the kind who can live with hardship and loss and be the stronger for it." I hadn't cried until then. Mr. Hobson put his arm around my shoulders. "There's nothing to be ashamed of in tears," he said gently. "James would be the first to tell us that."

November 17

It snowed in the night, covering our footprints and the track of the sled, and the grave. James's belongings have all been packed away. There's nothing to show that he was ever with us. The things he told me—about his father, about Sir John Ross, about Grace—are safe in my head. But is that all that's left of him here: a place in someone's mind?

Sam has broken his silence. Now I have someone to be with and to talk to, after a fashion. I'm not at ease with the others, I don't know why. Perhaps it's because James always understood so much of what I was thinking, without my having to find the right words for my thoughts. The others don't, not even Rob. He keeps trying to take my mind off it, suggesting distractions as if I were a child. But it doesn't help to be told, however kindly, "Don't brood about it."

November 30

A calm, bright night. The moon is almost full and the stars more brilliant than I've ever seen them. Even Polaris, which is usually so insignificant, is bright as a beacon tonight. The thermometer stands at 64 degrees below zero. Somewhere not far off a whole field of ice is moving. Even below decks you can hear it, a steady roar interrupted by low moans or sharp explosive cracks or noises like heavy wagons crawling uphill with ungreased axles.

Why do I feel so guilty about James? I wasn't responsible for the ice on deck. I didn't make him fall. But Mr. Hobson said that he thought a lot of me, and if that's right, I must have hurt him in those last few days. Silence can be like a wound. He gave me so much —his knowledge and his thoughts and his memories— and it must have seemed to him that I didn't care, that I threw it all away.

December 3

I found a little old-fashioned book at the back of the library shelf. *Devotions Upon Emergent Occasions,* by John Donne, Dean of St. Paul's. The *s*'s are shaped like *f*'s, and the cover is coming away from the spine. Someone read it once with a pen in his hand; whole paragraphs are underlined in brownish ink. One of the bits he marked was this:

> No man is an Island, entire of itself; every man is a piece of the Continent, a part of the main. If a clod be washed away by the sea, Europe is the less. . . . Any man's death diminishes me, because I am involved in Mankind.

But you could also say: any man's life enriches me, and for the same reason—"because I am involved in mankind." A part of me died when James died, it's true; but another part of me is more alive because he lived.

December 18

We have been kept busy building snow-houses and can now put one up in about three hours. The Captain says he won't be satisfied until we have it down to two hours or less. Cutting the blocks and fitting them together is comparatively quick and easy. It's chinking the cracks that takes the time.

The dogs have made several more attempts to board the ship. It seems to happen when the wheel-house light burns low or goes out. We've set two there now as a precaution.

December 20

Steve and Sy Smith have been groaning over a manual on *The Steam Engine, Theoretical and Practical.* Mr. Brands asked them to read it. I suppose that he wants them to take over James's work—one of them, at any rate. But I agree with Sy: those precise little diagrams, with their neat little captions, don't seem to have any bearing on the tangle of machinery down below. "Look at this," he said indignantly. " 'Surface condenser with three-quarter-inch brass tubes,' that's what it says. There's nothing like that on *this* ship, not that I've seen." He scowled at the illustration and relapsed into his usual silence.

December 25

Christmas Day—and my birthday, though no one knows it.

We had known that Cooky was preparing something special, from the sweet and spicy smells that drifted from the galley. Just how special it was to be, we hadn't guessed, because he wouldn't let anyone in except Dusty, and Dusty can keep a secret through any kind of teasing. Even the Chinese torture had no effect. He simply grinned and asked, "Didn't you ever 'ave wait-and-see puddin' at 'ome?" Of course I did. I used to ask, "What's for dinner?" and Mother would say, "Sausages and mash and pudding." "What kind of pudding?" "Wait and see." And that was all I'd ever get out of her: wait and see. "How did he come to let you in, anyway, Dusty?" " 'E needed someone to reach things off the top shelf." Since Cooky is a good head taller, that wasn't the reason. "No, really." "Well, you could say that it's because 'e's brewin' up a Cockney Christmas and needed some 'elp." "Are you a Cockney, then?" "Born within the sound of Bow Bells," he said proudly.

The fo'c'sle at noontime was a triumph, a glorious, bountiful dream of a Christmas dinner. There were apple pies and gooseberry pies and plum cakes and sponge cakes and raisin bread in shining braids and cream puffs and gingersnaps and a pyramid of buttery shortcake. And hams and cheeses and pickles and meat pies and golden-fried Scotch eggs. And nuts and chocolate and candied fruit. And beer and cider and rum-and-water. The ship's flags were swagged along the ceiling beams, silk sled banners decorated the bunks, and candles marched the length of the table, just visible above the mountains of food. If this is a Cockney Christmas, I'm moving to London.

The officers came down to see the spread and wished us merry Christmas with rum and plum cake. Later—much later—when we couldn't eat a crumb more and everything had been cleared away, we invited them back for carol singing. We sang all the carols we knew, and then we sang chanteys and ballads and marching songs. Finally we called on the Captain for a speech. "First," he said, "I would like to drink to the health of each and every one of you. I wish you all a merry Christmas and the best of fortune in the coming year. Second, I want to address myself to the fortunes of this expedition. We have met with bad luck, but let us hope that our luck will now turn, that we will soon reach our destination, and that we will find there what we seek. I give you a toast: Lady Franklin, whose courage and determination made this expedition possible." If James had been here, he would have replied to the Captain's speech and toasted him in turn. He was very good at that kind of thing. As it was, Old Harvey led us in the traditional three cheers. "And now three more for the Captain," he called. "Hip, hip, hurrah! hurrah! hurrah!"

In all the excitement, I almost forgot to open the package from Mother. There was a letter, a bag of walnuts, and a blank notebook bound in leather, with the endpapers marbled in a rainbow of colors. I've never had a grander diary. At the bottom of the package there were two pairs of socks with a pattern like a double twist of rope running up them. I would challenge any man to do work like that, whatever Rob may say about old Abbott and his shawls.

December 30

During December we drifted sixty-seven miles southeast, down Baffin Bay toward the Atlantic, and are now in latitude 74 degrees north.

January 1, 1858

We saw the New Year in with noise—you could hardly call it music. The flutes and the accordion did their best, but they were overwhelmed by the rest of the band. We had raided the galley and taken all the saucepans and their lids, a couple of tin trays, and Cooky's prized collection of wooden spoons. These made a considerable racket, but we also had all the whistles we could find—and the ship's bell. I think that the officers were a little appalled by the din, but the New Year is the New Year and only once, so they had to put up with it.

New Year's Resolutions.

Learn some more Eskimo—Sam is a long way ahead with *his* foreign language.

Be more tolerant of Raydon.

Keep the diary up to date.

Stop biting the nails—this is the third year for this particular resolution and it's time it was kept.

January 12

The doctor's reading class has droned its way to the end of a very dull treatise on trade winds. In ten long days that has been the only thing worth noting down.

January 17

Mr. Hobson and Mr. Young announced a competition in snow sculpture, with a prize—not specified—for the winner. I suspect that they aren't interested so much in art, as in getting us out into the fresh air. So now, as well as a ruined village of snow-houses, we have a statue gallery out there on the ice. The most ambitious piece is Rob's London Bridge. The towers are taller than he is and properly peaked and turreted with snow, but he is having trouble with the span itself. It keeps collapsing. He is thinking of using a piece of wood to reinforce it, but if he does he'll be disqualified. The rules state, "Material: snow; no foreign substances to be used," and no one has ever seen a tree growing in the pack. Anton, having watched for a while with a look of amazement on his face, set to and quickly made a seal. It is marvelously simple—just a smooth mound of snow with circles for the eyes and a few lines scored in for the flippers—but you know at once what it is. I'm doing a portrait of the Queen; it doesn't look like her at all.

January 18

The prize, a newfangled fur cap with earflaps, went to Raydon for his sphinx. I didn't think it was very good. The face was far too plump and pretty; it should have been angular and disdainful. Anton's seal was a much better thing altogether.

January 28

The sun is back. It was only a sliver, and we saw it for only a few minutes, but its return means the beginning of the end of winter. We greeted it with the yacht-club flag, a stuffed-looking red lion on a yellow ground.

February 19

Should Rob have told me? Alec thinks he shouldn't. And now that I know, what do I do with the knowledge? Tidy it away, to be looked at later? I can't do that.

Rob was shining the buttons on his best jacket. It was his birthday, he said, and he always shined himself up on that day, wherever he was and whatever else he had to do. I suddenly remembered that I'd never asked him what he meant by that strange remark about Doctor Rae and the things he brought back—the buttons and spoons and scraps of wood and metal. "Oh, that," he said. "That was a while back, now." He was hedging. I pressed him. "What about the buttons? What's important about them and the other things?" "You want me to tell you the whole story? Well, you may be sorry that you asked, but facts are facts and there's no denying them, so I'll tell you."

He spat on one of his buttons and rubbed it vigorously. "The odd thing is that the doctor wasn't looking for Franklin," he said. "He was out to add to the map, fill in the blank spaces around the south part of Boothia. Well, his name's on the map now: Rae Strait. That's where he was when he met these Eskimos. Like I said, he wasn't looking for Franklin, but he asked them anyway if they knew of any white men in those parts. They told him, 'No, not now, but four years ago our people saw some Europeans dragging sleds down the shore of King William Land. The Europeans were thin and looked hungry. And then later that year some bodies were found by our people, a long day's journey to the northwest, by the mouth of a great river.' That would be the Great Fish River, probably. Sometimes it's called Back's River, after the man who discovered it. Follow it far enough and it'll take you to the Hudson Bay trading posts, way inland."

"You were telling me about the white men that the Eskimos saw," I reminded him. "Were they from Franklin's expedition?" "Oh, yes, there's no doubt about that. The Eskimos had some things that proved it, and they gave them to the doctor. Or sold them, I don't know which. Coins and watches, naval buttons, brass ones, like these. Sir John's medals and . . ." "But that must mean that they're all dead," I interrupted. "No, it means that *some* of them are dead. No one knows for sure how the Eskimos got hold of those things, you see. Maybe they took them from the bodies at the Great Fish River. Or maybe there were other men besides the ones who died, and they traded the things with the Eskimos for food and then went on." "Up the river? inland to the trading posts?" "No one knows for sure," he repeated.

"But I don't see why you said that I would be sorry I asked about it." He looked at me speculatively. "It's not pleasant." "I'm not a child any more," I said. "I'm taller than you are now and a lot tougher than I used to be." "Well," said Rob, "one thing that the Eskimos told Doctor Rae was that the white men had eaten each other." The blood throbbed in my neck so hard that it was difficult to breathe. I didn't want to believe him, but I knew I had to. "Are you certain?" "Yes. It was cannibalism, heaven forgive them."

"You feeling alright? You look pale." It was Alec. "Rob just told me about those bodies by the Great Fish River," I said; I couldn't bring myself to say the word. "You mean about . . . He'd no right to tell you something like that." Alec was very upset. "It's true, isn't it?" I asked. "Oh, it's true enough, but it's something we all want to forget. I mean it." He turned to Rob. "Why did you have to bring it up again?" "It wasn't his fault," I said, trying to prevent a quarrel. "I made him tell me." Rob protested, "He's not a baby —and facts are facts." "Some facts are better buried," said Alec shortly. "Well, it's too late to bury this one," retorted Rob. "And I think that the boy has a right to know. It's something that has to be reckoned with."

Would I do it—eat a man I had known—if it meant the difference between living and dying? I don't think that I would or could; even the thought of it makes me retch. But how can I be sure? How strong *is* the instinct to live? Not knowing what it is like to be starving, I can't condemn what those men did. But I can't condone it either.

March 19

Yesterday we cleared the packed snow off the deck and the skylights, and there was sunlight below decks again. Even I was a bit shocked to see what a pigsty the fo'c'sle had become during the long dark days, and I'm not fussy about dirt or messiness. Every surface was grimed with smoke. The floor was greasy and crusted with old spills. There were spiders' webs between the beams and damp-stains in the corners. So today was spring-cleaning, and we scrubbed and wiped and polished until the place looked—and smelled—a bit more presentable.

April 6

LATITUDE 67° 18′ NORTH

The pack is splitting up fast, and we are separated from our old winter landmarks by thirty yards of open water. When the crack opened alongside the ship, she swung out into the water, and we had to pull her back before the ice moved again and slammed the lead shut. This took four hours, working in a howling gale and with the temperature well below zero. The hawsers were frozen stiff and useless; we had to haul out the chain cables to warp the *Fox* back into position.

April 8

Another split in the ice. Three boats and about half the dogs are cut off from us. The dogs are howling dismally, as if this is some new and uncalled-for punishment, but the water will freeze over tonight and they'll be able to get back. The boats are another problem. We have knapsacks and emergency supplies packed and are ready to desert the *Fox* at a moment's notice, if she is stove in by the ice. We might well need those three boats.

April 10

Alec, Davy, and Dusty rescued the boats and got back safely, though very wet and cold. They took a long roundabout route over the shifting ice and crept up on the runaways from behind.

April 20

The pack is battering itself to pieces. In the space of half an hour, a floe hundreds of yards across cracks and splits and smashes to fragments no bigger than a dinghy. The *Fox,* being part of the pack, is part of the battering, too. If she hadn't been doubled and fitted with those heavy crosspieces, she'd have been crushed long ago, and we would be out there with nothing but a cockle-shell of a boat between us and the ice.

It is "All hands on deck!" all the time now. The topmasts have been stepped and the yards sent aloft. Now we're working on the sails and the running gear. It's no fun lying out on the yard trying to bend a sail when the canvas is frozen stiff as glass and the rope has about as much flexibility as a piece of iron. The standing rigging, which of course has been out in the weather all winter, is cased in ice. We attack with belaying pins, yelling "Watch out, below there!" as the ice comes loose and crashes down. For a wonder, no one has been brained yet.

April 23

We are ready for the sea, and the sea is reaching out for us. You can see the swell running now under the broken ice. The crest rises five feet above the trough.

April 26

All day yesterday the swell rose and rose, until ten-foot waves of splintered ice were beating against the ship, setting the bells ringing and knocking us off our feet. We knew if the wind freshened and drove the swell higher, we'd be swamped. As if that were not enough to worry about, there were icebergs moving erratically through the pack. One came crashing toward us through the broken ice, a punch-drunk heavyweight pushing his way through a crowd. Just when I was certain that it would hit us—it was only a hundred feet away—it veered and went off to the north. It left a water space in its wake and the seas broke against it, hurling spray clear over its summit.

The Captain was on deck all day. He made a good

show of being unconcerned, but once, when he thought that no one was looking, he pounded his fist into the cupped palm of the other hand. I was glad that I wasn't in his shoes, making a decision that could send twenty-seven men to the bottom. As far as I could see, there were only two alternatives, and there was clear danger in both. We could stay as we were, hove-to, without steerage-way, and hope that we could withstand the battering we were getting. Or we could make sail and get up steam and try to force our way through the pack, knowing that a collision with the ice could damage the rudder or the propellor beyond repair. Just after midnight he made the decision: we would move.

He gave the orders calmly. "All hands stand by to ship the rudder . . . hoist the mainsail . . . the fore-top-sail . . . clear that block . . . ring down to the engineer . . . half speed ahead." Black smoke poured from the funnel, then thinned to a fine white plume. The *Fox* turned head on to the swell and slammed into the ice, staggering and wincing as she met it. We clung grimly to whatever handhold was nearest, and, when we had to move, crept by inches. Even so, the first impact sent us over like so many skittles. Lying there, with all the wind knocked out of me, I felt the boards of the deck buckle. It was a horrible sensation.

That was the first of many collisions, and not the worst, either. What happened next? I don't remember now. The day was one long confusion of noise and sudden violent movement, pain and bitter cold. I remember pitching headfirst across the fo'c'sle and landing, luckily, on a pile of foul-weather gear that had fallen to the floor, but I don't remember now when that was. And there was the time when ice clogged the propellor, the engines stopped dead, and the whole ship was filled with the sickening smell of burning oil. And another bad moment when some submerged obstacle wrenched the rudder around through ninety degrees and sent the helmsman reeling. But perhaps the worst of all was when the ship went completely out of control, spinning and lurching through the pack like a stick in a mountain riverbed when the spring flood is running.

By evening the swell had risen to thirteen feet and was rolling fast, but the ice was looser, and we could see clear spaces of water ahead. It became possible to steer around the larger pieces of ice. We began to put on speed. At eight bells we were out of the pack, running through its ragged edges into the open sea. No one had the strength left to cheer, but you could read relief and triumph in everyone's face. The order was given to stop the engines. Mr. Brands had been on duty for eighteen hours without a break. He is the only one, now that James is dead, who knows how to work the engines. I saw him later. Sweat had dug pink channels through the grime on his skin. He was too tired to clean up.

April 28

Our winter set a record—not a very cheerful one. We were in the ice for 242 days and during that time drifted 1,385 miles, zigzagging down Baffin Bay in the general direction of the Atlantic. This is the longest drift known.

August 11

BEECHEY ISLAND

It has been three and a half months since my last entry in this diary. So much for my resolution to keep it up to date.

After we broke free from the pack, we headed back to Greenland. At Holsteinsborg we took on fresh water, which was very welcome, and a huge quantity of rock cod, which was not. From there we went south to Godhavn, where I got sick. The doctor said he thought it was food poisoning, but the only thing I ate that no one else had was some pickled whaleskin that a Danish girl gave me and I would hate to think that she was responsible. That was in May. By the middle of June we were back at the top of Baffin Bay, making a second attempt to get through to the North Water. This time we had better luck, found the water comparatively clear, and made the crossing in two weeks.

We picked up a gale at the entrance to Lancaster Sound and came in fast and rough, dodging small icebergs. Now we're lying in a glassy calm off Beechey Island, whistling for a wind. Wellington Channel stretches away to the north, with the granite cliffs of Cornwallis Island as a background for its unrippled blue. I wish that I could draw.

Today I rowed the Captain over to what he grandly calls Beechey Island House, though it's not much more than a broken-backed hut, half-filled with snow where the door has blown in. A depot was left here by the last Franklin search party when they sailed for home four years ago. We found a lifeboat whose paintwork was as fresh as if it were still wet, some paddles and oars, extra clothes, and provisions of all kinds. Among these was a five-pound tin of syrup, just like the one we had at home. It gave me a jolt to see it there, with its familiar green and gold lettering. The Captain looked over the stores, decided that the biscuit was spoiled, but that we could use the syrup, part of the case of chocolate, and some of the clothes. It seems that, in the Arctic, you take what you need and leave what you can. Were these things left here in the hope that Franklin's men would find and use them?

The plan is to sail from here into Peel Strait and to follow it southward toward King William Land, leaving Somerset Land to port. This is the track that the *Erebus* and *Terror* must have taken; all the other possible routes have been searched and nothing has been found. We must be close now to success. If only there were a wind!

August 18

Peel Straight was blocked with ice. A dead end. We turned about and are now circling back around Somerset Land looking for a passage called Bellot Strait. Bellot Strait is our last chance of getting through to the western sea and King William Land, but it is marked on the chart with a hesitant dotted line and may not be there at all.

Could the *Erebus* and *Terror* have got through Peel Strait, if the *Fox* couldn't? Rob says they might well have made it. "You can't tell from season to season where you'll find the ice," he said. "Why, I remember coming into Lancaster Sound one year and the ice looked as solid as if it had been lying there since the day of Creation and meant to stay until the Last Judgment. And the next year there wasn't a chip in sight. . . . Ice is as fickle as a woman," he added sourly.

August 20

LATITUDE 72° NORTH

The map-makers can join the dots and make a solid line and mark it "Bellot Strait." It would be easy enough to miss it, though. It is very narrow, hardly more than a split in the cliffs, and the entrance is hidden by a jumble of little islands. We landed an emergency cache today at the eastern outlet of the strait, and tomorrow we will go through. Tomorrow we will be in the western sea. I can see the headlines in the newspapers: SUCCESS AT LAST . . . FRANKLIN FOUND . . . MC CLINTOCK WINS THROUGH.

August 21

Halfway through the strait the ice stopped us. We could see waves breaking on the cliffs at the western end, only ten miles away—ten miles that might as well have been a thousand. Then the tide turned like a sluice-gate opening and swept us back. All the way back.

August 25

Another attempt on Bellot Strait. With all sail set, the engines thudding and the tide with us, we got clear through—and found ourselves fenced in at the western end by unbroken acres of pack ice.

This is like playing Snakes and Ladders. You work your way tediously to the top of the board (in this game it's called Bellot Strait) and then an unlucky throw puts you on square 99 and you slither down the biggest snake of them all right back to the beginning.

September 15

Captain McClintock doesn't give up easily. He took us into Bellot Strait three more times before he admitted himself beaten and forced to winter here, at the *eastern* end of that wretched narrows.

We are tucked safely into a little bay, which the Captain named Port Kennedy, double-anchored and snugged down for the winter. A shoulder of land lies between us and the worst of the wind that comes roaring down the strait, but nothing can keep the fog away. It is black, this fog, full of flying splinters of ice that whip your skin until it is raw. The only thing to do is to try to cover your face completely with overlapping layers of mufflers and caps, not very practical when you have to see where you are going. Sam has a pair of goggles made out of wood, quite thick and with the narrowest possible eye slits. I shall try to make myself a pair, if I can persuade Jackson to part with that piece of mahogany he is hoarding "in case it comes in useful."

Little Dolly, who is not much more than a puppy herself, gave birth to a litter of four the day we landed. It was as if she had been waiting for a little peace and quiet—and some solid ground under her heaving sides—before undertaking this early motherhood. Davy trundled the barrel-kennel out onto the shore. It hasn't been used since Pip's brothers and sisters grew up.

September 20

Raydon asked me to fetch Doctor Walker. He said he felt "seedy," and I must say he looked it.

There was no one in the officers' mess. A chart was spread out on the table, surrounded by a clutter of pencils and protractors and scraps of paper with figures scribbled on them. I couldn't resist looking. Our present position was inked in in red, "Port Kennedy." From that point three lines radiated out, striking boldly into the blank spaces of the map. *Terra Incognita.* Unknown country. Someone coughed behind me. It was Mr. Hobson. I hadn't heard him come in. "I was looking for Doctor Walker, sir," I explained. "I thought you were looking at the chart," he retorted, laughing. "Well, yes, it sort of caught my eye," I admitted.

"These lines are the tracks proposed for the spring sled expeditions," he said, tracing them with his finger. "We'll be setting out soon with the advance depots." "Depots, sir?" "That's the Captain's own idea, and a very good one, too. With a secure advance depot, you can double the range of any expedition." "I don't quite see . . ." I said, puzzled. "It's not too complicated. First you decide where you are going to go. It's a final decision, no room for second thoughts. Then you take supplies out along the route, as far out as you can. You bury them deep, beyond the reach of bears, and mark the place so that you will be able to find it again. This is what we'll be doing in the next few weeks, laying an advance depot on each of these three routes. Here, maybe, and here and here." He picked up a pencil and drew three faint circles across the lines on the map. "The main expeditions will leave in the spring. They will set out with a full load, pulling as much as they can. By the time they reach the depots, their supplies will be getting low, so they'll take what they need from the cache and push on." "This was the Captain's idea?" "Yes, it's one of those things that seems so obvious that you wonder why no one thought of it before. But no one did." "Has he tried it out, to see if it works?" I asked. "Last time he was in the Arctic, yes. But never over distances like these." He swept his hand across the chart. The words jumped out at me again: *Terra Incognita.*

I remembered why I had come to the mess. "Do you know where the Doctor is, sir?" "He's out with the dogs, doing some surgery on ears and paws and such. Didn't you hear them fighting?" I had heard them of course, but I'd kept away. Dogfights turn my stomach to water and my legs to jelly.

Doctor Walker was putting the last stitch in a long tear on Omar's hip. Omar is the smallest of the males and always runs away from trouble if he can. This time he hadn't run hard enough: it was a nasty wound. The dog's jaws were bound together with a thong, and he was squirming wildly, even though Sam was holding him down with all his weight. I told the Doctor that Raydon wanted to see him. "What's his trouble? Is it urgent?" he wanted to know. "He says he feels seedy, sir." "Tell him I'll be by when I've finished patching up these brawling Greenlanders, will you?" I delivered the message to Raydon. He seemed no worse, but no better either.

September 22

A clear day. No fog and no wind for a change. We built a large house of ice blocks on the shore for an observatory. Rob drove stakes into the snow and looped a rope between them to mark the way, even though it's no real distance. It was as well he did. The fog came down again in the evening, and when Old Harvey went out to make the first reading of the declinometer, he walked into invisibility with three paces.

The Doctor has been cross-questioning Raydon about his diet—what he likes to eat, what he never touches. It seems that Raydon has never eaten any of the preserved meat or vegetables; he's been subsisting all this time on salt "horse." I don't know how he could stand it.

September 23

Raydon has scurvy. That's why there were so many questions about his food, then. It's his own fault, but I can't help feeling sorry for him. His gums are terribly inflamed, and even swallowing is painful. His prescription is a double dose of lemon juice. He grumbles about taking it. "These young doctors, they think they know everything. I've managed for years without this stuff. Didn't do me any harm." And so on. Alec said, with unnecessary roughness, "Perhaps young doctors know more about medicine than old sailors." I think he's a bit scared by the scurvy—and I'm not sure that I'm not scared too. Raydon has been very stupid, but the seeds of the disease may be in all of us.

October 12

Nine of us are to go with Mr. Hobson to advance a depot down the west coast of Boothia as near to King William Land as we can. We'll be leaving sometime next week with four sleds and ten of the dogs. " 'E's tellin' us now, so as we 'ave time to get our socks washed out!" said Dusty.

Dolly's puppies are not thriving. Sam says that they should be taken away from her, even though they are a little young to be on their own. "She has little milk and little fur," he said. He took a dish of bread scraps mixed with water and some seal's blood out to the kennel, but Dolly ate it all herself before the puppies had time to scramble to their feet.

October 14

A hair-raising shriek from the galley. Cooky had opened a new cask of biscuit and found a mouse in it. He explained hastily that he had yelled out because he was surprised, not having seen a single mouse on board before. The little creature must have been there since the cask was packed more than a year ago. Ship's biscuit is very dry feeding, but it's obviously nutritious: the mouse was full grown and very lively. It was half an hour before we caught it. I put it in a tin, with a good supply of its favorite food. I was going to give it some water, but Alec stopped me. "It's not accustomed to drink, see. Water would go straight to its head—like whiskey would to yours." Perhaps he's right, but I can't help thinking how dry I'd be after a year in a biscuit barrel.

October 17

We were to have left this morning, but a violent northwester was blowing. No one went outdoors all day, except the men on observatory duty. The declinometer has to be read every hour on the hour, whatever the weather.

October 18

The mouse escaped from its tin and vanished. Not a whisker to be seen. I thought I heard it scuttling around under the deck, but there are so many noises at night that I couldn't be sure.

November 7

We left the *Fox* on October 19, very early—Mr. Hobson, eight men, and me. The sleds had been loaded the night before. There were five hundred pounds of supplies on each of the dog-sleds and rather more than that on the sleds we were to pull. Sam hitched up the dogs, and the men assigned to the first lap shrugged on their traces. We went along the strait, skirting the water, and turned south. It was a forced march, through deep snow. We never stopped, except to untangle the dogs' harnesses. After hours and hours, Mr. Hobson gave the order to make camp. We pitched the tents, working in a wind that came straight from the Pole, and carried into them everything that the dogs could possibly destroy—harnesses, spare clothing, blankets, food in wooden boxes, every scrap of leather or cloth. When that was done, we swallowed a tepid meal, eased off our frozen boots, and wriggled into the blanket bags.

If anything, it was worse in the blanket bags. The wind tore through the tent flaps, and the frost struck up from the ground through the bedding. Nothing had prepared me for it. The cold, I mean. The real Arctic. Always before, there had been the ship for shelter, a warm dry bunk, the fo'c'sle stove, and hot food from the galley. This time there was no relief.

The next five days and nights were like the first. We went on down the coast of Boothia, marching hard all day and camping at night on the shore—and getting colder and colder, if that were possible. On the sixth day out, we came to rugged mountain country, too rough for the sleds, and took to the sea ice. That night we pitched the tents on the edge of the pack. In the small hours the wind changed and starting blowing off-shore. Dusty was on watch and gave the alarm at once, but it was too late. The ice had broken away and we were drifting out to sea. We packed up the tents, our only protection from the wind, and sat on the sleds

all night squinting into the driving snow for a chance to escape.

In the gray light of the next morning we saw that our piece of ice was getting smaller. Bit by bit the edges broke off until it was no more than forty feet wide. We huddled in the middle, holding the dogs, afraid to move. If the ice split again, everything would be over for us. The sleds were too heavily loaded to float. No one could live for more than a few seconds in that water. There was nothing we could do except wait—for the end or for a miracle.

They say that at moments like that, when death may be only minutes away, your whole life passes in front of your eyes. All day I expected this to happen, but I saw nothing except the cold gray sea, the raft of ice, and the snow falling so thickly that it was a solid sheet of white.

In the evening, the ice drifted across the mouth of an inlet and grounded—it must have been thicker than we had supposed. There was still a quarter-mile of water between us and safety, but that night the thermometer dropped even lower, and a bridge of salt ice formed. Being by far the lightest, I tested it first. The ice swayed and cracked alarmingly, but it held. We unpacked the sleds and divided up the gear and provisions into small loads, not more than a few pounds each. Then we crept back and forth between the floe and the shore, one man at a time, until everything was ferried over. The dogs were last, galloping happily across with the empty sleds swinging behind them.

We established the depot in latitude 71 degrees

north, about ninety miles from the ship. The stores and supplies were buried at the foot of a huge boulder, and we built a cairn of stones over them. They should be easy enough to find.

On the second night of the return journey, Mr. Hobson, furious with Sophie for chewing up her harness, ordered a muzzle put on her. The next morning I found her lying dead in her own blood. The other dogs had attacked her, avenging some old grudge perhaps, and she had been too tightly gagged to defend herself. She hadn't even been able to bark; the whole thing had happened in silence. Without their leader, her team started to bicker and quarrel and fall behind in the march. Once, when I was driving them, a real fight broke out. The gray dog, Rolf, started it, lunging at his neighbor's throat for no reason that I could see. All my old fear came back. I couldn't move, but I knew I had to. If I didn't do something, and do it fast, there would be another dog dead. Somehow I made myself edge up to Rolf, pry his mouth open, and drag him off. He looked up at me, angry still but openly astonished. I was astonished myself.

We got back yesterday, the sixth. In all the time that we were gone from the ship, I never saw a sign of any wild thing, not even a print in the snow or the mess of feathers that shows where a fox has killed. Nothing moved in that white land except the figures of the men in front of me and the straggling dog-teams. Yet Eskimos have lived out their lives here. We found circles of stones where their huts had been and charred rocks where they had had a cook-fire. Somehow they found game and cooked it and endured that bitter cold. If they survived, so could Franklin's men—and so can I. But there were times during those eighteen days when all I wanted to do was to lie down and never move again.

November 8

Mr. Brands died today. Or, rather, some time last night. Mike found him on the cabin floor when he went to call him for breakfast. The Doctor thinks it was apoplexy. "It must have been that," he said. "There's nothing else that strikes so suddenly, without warning."

Mr. Brands was a very lonely man, I think. He always took a walk at mid-day, whatever the weather, trudging along all by himself with his hands clasped behind his back. Perhaps the engineer on an auxiliary sailing ship is always lonely. The other officers don't understand pistons and valves and steam pressure. They're tuned to wind and canvas and resent the flat calm that gives him his chance to shine. We buried him on the shore at the foot of the cliff.

Now there is no one on board who knows how to run the engines. Steve Smith is still on chapter two of *The Steam Engine,* and Sy, though he finished the manual a while ago, says despairingly that he is no wiser than he was when he began it. At the moment we've no need for steam, or sails either, but when the ice breaks up it will be a different story. And then what will happen?

November 15

I set three fox traps in the rocks and baited them with some scraps of salt "horse" saved from dinner. If I can catch a fox and cure the skin and make a fur vest—shades of Robinson Crusoe!—I may be able to endure the cold a bit better. My coat is double-thick wool, but the wind goes through it as if it were cheesecloth. Another thing I must do is to get that wood from Jackson and copy Sam's snow goggles.

November 17

Nothing has been near the traps. I changed the bait. Maybe I'll have better luck with seal meat, but I doubt it. There are no prints in the snow except for the spidery little tracks of the ptarmigan.

The sea is as deserted as the land. Sam set nets for seals weeks ago and has caught nothing.

December 20

For five days we haven't stirred out of doors because of the wind and the cold. It was 80 degrees below zero last night. The air in the fo'c'sle is stale and sour with tobacco smoke. Everyone is short-tempered. There's nothing to do. The old hands have told their stories so often that we know them all by heart. Only mealtime breaks the monotony.

December 25

The Christmas feast was less lavish than last year's. To make up for the lack of variety in the menu, Cooky let himself go with the pastry cutter. He made shields and ships, roses and anchors, and a number of unidentifiable animals, all glazed a shiny brown—and all rather tough. The centerpiece was a remarkably buxom mermaid with braided hair, made of a sweet bread-dough. Cooky said sadly, "She rose more than I thought she would."

My presents from Mother were a painted metal penbox that had rusted so badly that I couldn't even open it, and a book—Charles Dickens' new one, *Hard Times*. The pages are all warped and spotted with the damp and the red dye on the cover has run. I wonder why she chose that particular title. Did she mean it as some kind of joke?

Altogether it wasn't a very good Christmas or a good birthday either.

January 1, 1859

This year will see the end of the search for Franklin. If all goes well.

Looking back at last year's resolutions, I find that I didn't keep one of them. I'm still snapping at Raydon. I'm still biting my nails. Sam has outstripped me so far that I've given up trying to learn Eskimo, it's so much easier to speak English. As for the diary—since that long lapse in the summer, I've done better, but not as well as I could. I'm only going to make one resolution for 1859: to do the best I can.

January 10

The Captain and Mr. Young picked their teams for next month's sled expeditions. Alec and Mr. Petersen are to go with the Captain down to the south of Boothia to try to make contact with the Eskimos. Mr. Young plans to cross the western sea to Prince of Wales

Land, where Franklin may have left some trace behind. Dusty, Davy, and Sam are to go with him. The rest of us are to stay here. I wish that I were going—on either expedition, it wouldn't matter which. Anything would be better than this, even the cold.

February 18

I'm to be in charge of Dolly and the puppies while Sam is away. It will give me something to do and an excuse to get out of the fo'c'sle from time to time. There always seems to be an argument going on, usually about the food or the weather. It's because we've all been cooped up together for so long, of course, but knowing that doesn't make it any easier to avoid taking sides and saying things that I regret the moment I've said them. I foresee that the puppies will most need attention when Raydon starts one of his long querulous speeches. Nff, nff.

February 23

The problem with the puppies, as with the older dogs, is to see that each gets his fair share of the food. We cut up their meat and scatter it broadcast on the ice, trying to equalize their chances; but the strong get stronger all the time at the expense of the weak. The weakest of the puppies is called Victor. I don't know who named him: he's a loser if ever I saw one. Today all he had for dinner was a lick of the ice where a piece of meat had been lying. I took a little extra food out to him later and stood over him while he ate it, bolting it down as if he had to do ten days' eating in as many minutes.

March 3

Mr. Young and his party returned today. Prince of Wales Land was barren of any trace of man, English or Eskimo.

March 10

A fox in the trap at last, when I had given up hope. The fur is very long, silver gray. I feel warmer just looking at it. Sam helped me flay and scrape the skin. I was making a botch of it, working by myself.

March 14

The Captain's team is back. All three of them look pinched and thin. Alec told us about it, holding court by the stove with a great mug of hot grog warming his hands.

"The dogs went lame on the third day out. They tracked blood on the snow, their paws were cut so deep. I mean it. They're alright now, but it held us up. We had to nurse them along, see. Do their share of the hauling as well as our own. After two weeks we were miles from where we'd hoped to be and getting to the end of the rations for the outward trip. And we still hadn't seen a single Eskimo. Not one. Then I looked behind me, and there were four men tailing us. They might have been there for days, they move so quietly. I mean it. The Captain and Mr. Petersen buckled on their pistols and went back to meet them. They were from Cape Victoria, part of the tribe we were looking for. One of them asked after Sir John Ross—Agglugga, he called him. He'd been Ross's guide. It's a small world, even up here.

The next day they took us to their village. I tell you —no offense to you, Sam—those women are plain. Faces like suet puddings. They have pretty hands though. There were a lot of things from Franklin's ships in the village. Sled runners made from barrel staves. A fair amount of wood and metal. Brass buttons that they'd sewn on the hems of their dresses. The Captain bought everything they had. He paid for them

with knives and needles. The needles were for the women, see, and the girls. One woman got five or six. She bargained away everything she could and ripped her dress pulling the buttons off. When she'd got nothing left to trade, she took her baby out of her dress and held it out to the Captain. It was stark naked, the poor little thing, and the temperature well below zero. You should have seen the Captain's face. She wanted another needle, see, and she got it—double-quick.

Well, anyway. Mr. Petersen asked them where they got the things. They said, on an island where there are salmon. That means a river. Back's Great Fish River, probably." He looked at me sidelong. The breath stuck in my throat, just as it did when Rob first told me what had happened there. Alec went on, "Then Mr. Petersen asked them about the ships. Had they seen two ships anywhere? An old man spoke up. There had been a three-masted ship, he said, a long time ago. She'd been crushed by the ice and sunk, see, and the people had gone on foot to the river. He drew some lines on the snow with his spear. That was where the ship went down, he said, and stabbed a hole. We couldn't make head or tail of his drawing, or map, or whatever it was. Did he know anything about another ship? No, he said, this was the only one, and he stabbed at the hole again."

So one of the ships is accounted for, crushed and sunk, and her crew dead on the island where the salmon are. The other may still be afloat and the men alive somewhere.

Alec said nothing about the cold, I realize now, and

it must have been terrible, far worse than in November. His fingers and toes are frostbitten, and his face too, but he never said a word about it.

March 15

Until yesterday, when Alec came back with his mixed bag of news, I'd had no doubt that we would succeed. We would find the men—some of them anyway—and the ships, and sail victoriously back home. But now I'm not sure at all. I think that I have been refusing to look reality in the face. What real hope is there that any of the men have survived? And if they are alive, what are our chances of finding them? They could be anywhere within hundreds of miles. And the ships: one has gone down and there's not even a rumor of what might have happened to the other. Today those newspaper headlines read, ANOTHER FAILURE . . . NO TRACE OF FRANKLIN . . . MC CLINTOCK ACKNOWLEDGES ATTEMPT UNSUCCESSFUL.

March 16

I was much too pessimistic yesterday. Lady Franklin must have thought that there was a chance, or she wouldn't have sent the expedition out. What did she say in that letter? Our mission was to rescue any possible survivor of the *Erebus* and *Terror,* to bring back the documents of Franklin's expedition, and to confirm his discovery of the Northwest Passage. If Captain McClintock thought that these were impossible goals, would he have accepted the command? I don't think he would.

If there are no survivors of the *Erebus* and *Terror,* then are the documents really so important? "Of course they are," said Rob. "That's a half-witted question. If the men are dead, the documents are the only way we can know what happened." "But if they're dead, that's all we need to know, isn't it?" "There's more to it than that," Alec said. "Look, if anything happened to me, Betty would want to know about it. What I was doing; if I died bravely. Things like that. So that she could say to herself, he died in a good cause. And that would help her, see. Now I don't say those men are dead, but if they are, there's hundreds of wives who don't know what happened. Those sailors died gallantly, doing their duty, you can be sure of that. Their people should know it." "And all that would be in the documents?" "Well," said Alec, "there'd be papers—letters and diaries and the like. They'd tell." "They'd not tell a thing if the ship went down with all hands." Raydon took the gloomy view as always.

"Alec's thinking of his Betty, of course," said Rob. "I haven't got a wife, never had one, never will have one, either, if I can help it. So perhaps I look at this differently. You've been talking about diaries and letters. But there would be charts and maps and log-books, too; the records of the expedition. If we had those, we'd know where they went, and if they found the Northwest Passage. Now don't you ask me if that's important! You know it is, and if you didn't, you wouldn't be here. Some people live their lives in the cabbage patch and never look beyond the fence. You could explain to them why finding the Northwest Passage is important—explain and explain until you were blue in the face—and they'd never understand. You're not one of those, nor is Alec or the Captain or any of us here."

March 18

The officers spent all day rummaging around for three casks of sugar that have inexplicably disappeared. When they had gone through the entire ship and the stores that we landed on the beach in the fall and were still unsuccessful, they asked for volunteers to go to Fury Beach and pick up some sugar from the depot there. I said that I would go, but the Captain refused. "I'm counting on you for the spring sled expedition," he said. "Save your energy for that." I'm both disappointed and flattered, a fine mixture. Disappointed that he wouldn't let me go, flattered that he should have chosen me.

March 24

The foxes and the ptarmigan are still in white, but today I saw a lemming in its brown coat. One sign of spring! The other was the order given by Old Harvey, at the top of his lungs: "All hands to the shovels!" We cleared the *Fox* of her snow embankment and chipped the dirty ice off the deck.

There's much more to making a vest than I'd thought. For one thing, I found I hadn't enough fur and had to use part of an old pair of trousers as well. For another, the fox skin resisted both scissors and needles. I had to cut it with a knife and punch it with a bradawl. The result of my afternoon's tailoring is a most extraordinarily lumpy and uncomfortable garment that looks as if it had been thrown together by someone with a bad temper and two left hands. I don't think I'll ever wear it.

March 26

There was sugar in the tea this morning, but it was not come by easily. Mr. Young and Dusty are blind as kittens from the glare, and Anton is only a little better off. The blindness began to come on a couple of days after they started back from Fury Beach, Dusty said, and at about the same time one of the sleds broke down.

They piled all the sugar, eight hundred pounds of it, on the other sled. With a load like that, of course, it would run only on smooth ice; in the hummocks and the rough places it was worse than useless. They had to unload the sugar, carry it to the next stretch of good ice, manhandle the sled over the hummocks, and load up again. "It wasn't so bad while we could see. But when we couldn't any longer, and Anton 'ad to lead us every step of the way, 'alf blind 'imself and not knowin' enough of the language to warn us . . . Well, I don't want to go through that again."

March 30

Only three more days and we'll be off on the long sled journey—the final journey and the end of the search, one way or the other.

Doctor Walker will stay with the *Fox*. Cooky, Jackson, and Raydon will be left behind too—Cooky and Jackson because there is work for them here, Raydon because he is ill. He looks very ill indeed. I've sometimes wondered whether he takes the lemon juice or whether he just tips it on to the floor. But not to take it is suicide.

The rest of us are divided into three teams. The names were posted yesterday. Mr. Hobson has Dusty, Davy, the Smith brothers, and Anton as driver. Rob,

Alec, Mr. Petersen, and I are in the Captain's party, and Sam drives our dogs. Everyone else goes with Mr. Young. Each team is to take a dogsled and a man-hauled sled.

The Captain has been busy with his spring-balance, weighing and checking and adding. "Provisions—930 pounds. Tent, sleeping bags, floorcloth—90 pounds. Pots and pans and tools—50 pounds. That seems rather high. See if you can find a small saw instead of this one. Magnetic and astronomical instruments—60 pounds. Heavy, but essential." The total for each team is supposed to come to no more than 1,400 pounds, which is enough to haul, goodness knows! My knapsack of spare clothes weighed in at 15 pounds. It should have been about 10 and I was sent back to repack it. "I'll let you have a few extra ounces," said the Captain. "You will need a pen and a fair-sized bottle of ink if you are to keep your diary up to date. We will be away for more than two months, don't forget." How ever did he know about my diary? I wasn't going to take it, but since he knows about it, I will. I jettisoned two pairs of socks and a sweater and packed the diary instead. My knapsack was still too heavy, but he let it pass.

April 1—Fool's Day

We leave tomorrow—no fooling!

April 2

In honor of the occasion, the *Fox* flew her yacht-club flag, and the silk banners were fastened to the loaded sleds. Ours was red, with the name FRANKLIN in white letters and a margin of white embroidery. It was very trig and brave—and incongruously feminine. Since our route was the same for quite a distance, Mr. Hobson's team and ours left together: twelve men, seventeen dogs, and five sleds. *Five* sleds because at the last moment the Captain decided to take lame Omar and Dolly and her starveling puppies, though they had never been yoked before. What might have been an impressive departure became a confusion of barks and squeals and shouts, as the puppies went through every trick they knew to avoid the whip and the work. The Captain drove them himself. Somehow he managed to keep them going in the same direction as the rest and at about the same speed.

The ice in Bellot Strait was very rough, churned by the tides racing through below. We took the "high road" up to the hills and trekked over a frozen lake lying parallel with the strait. The sleds were heavy and the snow deep in the hollows. We made only a few miles before we camped for the night. I noticed the Captain thawing out his ink over the cook-stove and was glad that I'd brought a pencil. He is still writing now, filling in the logbook, I suppose. His shadow on the tent roof is like a great eagle, his shoulders its hunched wings and his nose its beak.

April 4

In the western sea, the ice is smooth as a duck pond. This morning we hoisted the square sled sails and ran southward before the wind with the dogs chasing along behind. The Captain must have been glad of this respite from his struggles with the puppy team. Yesterday they discovered that they were safe from the whip if they hid under the sled.

April 16

Snow blindness comes on gradually, I know now. For two or three days my eyes were sore and dry, as if I'd been reading too late by a smoky light. I didn't worry about it. But then my vision began to blur, the whole landscape became a swimming sea of white, and the pain began. My eyeballs were huge, throbbing, red-hot. The light was agony. I tried to draw down the lids to cool my eyes and shut out the light, but they were lined with sandpaper and rasped when I moved them. The Captain wrapped a dark cloth around my head and yoked me shoulder to shoulder with Rob. He talked me across the roughest ice we've come to yet—or did it only seem that way?

The bandage came off this evening. To my new eyes, the men seem very small and frail, no match at all for the land and the weather. Already the snow glare and the cold have disfigured them. Their faces are blistered, their eyes inflamed, and their lips and fingers cracked to the raw flesh.

April 17

We found our advance depot easily enough and are now pulling a full load again. From this point—latitude 71° 7′ north by the Captain's calculations—the land runs south straight as a ruler and as flat. It is oddly quiet. Apart from the noise of our marching, the only sound is a whispering like wind in dry grass as the ice shifts with the tide.

Rob's and Alec's eyes are painful now, even though they have been wearing spectacles with colored lenses.

Only Sam, peering out through the narrow slits of his goggles, seems immune from snow blindness. I was a fool not to finish my goggles while there was still time. I'll never get them done now.

April 18

We buried a depot (pemmican, biscuit, two pistols, ammunition, kerosene) to be picked up on the return journey. The cairn that marks it is conspicuous for miles, too conspicuous, perhaps. We tried to place the rocks with their weathered faces to the outside, but it didn't always work. The cairn is obviously new and obviously built for a purpose. If I were an Eskimo, I'd want to know what that purpose was. I'd pull down the cairn. The depot would be exposed. And Alec says that they are natural-born thieves.

April 22

LATITUDE 70° 30′ NORTH

Alec was right; partly right anyway. In our terms they are shameless thieves, but it seems that our terms are not theirs. Sam said, "With the Eskimo people, is like this. I need to cut: I take the knife. You need to fish: you take the net. It is for who needs it." This was by way of explaining the disappearance of a tin saucepan from the load on our sled. We had a saucepan—they needed a saucepan—they took the saucepan. It was as simple as that. Where everything is scarce, food and tools and everything else, maybe it must be that simple.

We met the Eskimos two days ago almost a mile offshore, seal-hunting on the edge of the ice. They are from the same village that the Captain and Mr. Petersen and Alec visited in February. There are two families, one of them headed by the old man who drew the map in the snow to show where the ship went down. He recognized Alec at once, "Although," he said, "he is fatter now." At least, that's how Sam translated it; but there seemed to be more to it than that, because the old man laughed heartily. "Fatter," meaning perhaps "fat enough"? I still can't quite face the thought of Englishmen being cannibals. Perhaps it was the Eskimos? But that seems just as incredible.

Oonalee, the old man, invited us into his snowhouse. He apologized for it, saying that if he had known we were coming, he would have built much bigger and better, that this was only a temporary camp and not fit for guests and so on. But after all that practice last winter, I know good snow architecture when I see it. This house is beautifully made. The entrance passage, sited downwind, is low, but not so low that you have to crawl. It leads to a round hall full of nets and spears and other gear, the storeroom evidently. Two passages branch out from the hall, widen to form larders, and come out into the main rooms. These are maybe twelve feet across and over eight feet high at the top of the dome. The inside walls are hard ice, the kind of ice that only forms if all the cracks are well chinked.

We sat down where Oonalee pointed, on a mound of reindeer skins at the back of the room. Several members of his family squatted beside us. The skins were soft and smelled rancid. An old woman, who had been tending her stone cooking-lamp, bustled out to the larder and brought us thin strips of frozen blubber. I hesitated, but the Captain hissed at me, "Take it and smile." Chewing on this delicacy as politely as I could, I looked around.

It wasn't easy to see. There was a slab of ice set in the dome, for a window, but the light it let in was almost drowned by black oily smoke rolling up from the cooking lamp. Fur mittens and leggings hung drying on a rack over the lamp. There were some seal's intestines in a stone bowl. Oonalee's supper? The old woman's work, a strip of fox fur, was on the floor. She picked it up and began to chew on it. Oonalee looked at her approvingly. Mr. Petersen translated his comment: "She is a good woman and a good worker. I will have soft fur for my boots." He is a good worker himself: it was warm in the snowhouse, almost too warm.

The Captain was looking around, too. I saw his gaze fix on a knife that Oonalee's eldest son wore at his waist. "May I see that knife?" he asked. Mr. Petersen translated the question, and the young man handed the knife to the Captain. I saw that the blade was marked with a broad arrow—the official government

stamp. "Ask him, please, where he got this." There was a long muttered conversation, and then Mr. Petersen said, "He picked it up on a shore where a ship is stranded. It was then this long." He stretched out his arm. "After, he broke it up small to make knives." "Tell him that I will buy the knife, and ask if he knows more about the ship he mentioned." The conversation began again. A sudden movement attracted my attention to Oonalee. The old man was glaring at his son as he talked with the interpreter. Obviously something was being said that the father would have preferred kept secret. "There were *two ships,*" said Mr. Petersen at last. "One sank in deep water. These people got nothing from that one. They are sorry for that. The other ship grounded at Ootloolik, that is what they call the place. The knife and other things come from there." "And the men from the ships?" "They went to the island where there are salmon, the large river, like the old man said before. This man says the ship was still at Ootloolik when they went there last time, but broken, very broken."

Why did the old man not mention the other ship, when they talked to him in February? Alec was certain that he had not. "He jabbed his spear in the snow and said that there was only the one ship." Why was he so angry with his son for telling us about it? Is there something at Ootloolik that he doesn't want us to find?

April 23

Alec says that it was Oonalee's wife who pulled her baby out of her dress that cold February day to beg an extra needle. I thought she was an *old* woman. But then, they are all so muffled in furs and blackened by lamp smoke that it is hard to tell a girl from her grandmother. At least I can tell man from woman: the women have tattooed lines on their cheeks, and the men have their hair cut short at the back.

Oonalee has been asking all day about the *Fox*—where she is, how many people are there, what provisions are on board. I think he would be off to Port Kennedy if he had a chance, but the Captain has bought his two dogs and he can't go so far on foot with his large family. Which is just as well. It would be a pity if the master builder became a beggar like his wife.

April 27

CAPE VICTORIA

Some abandoned snow-houses and an old sled mark the site of the village; the people have moved on. "This is very old way of working," Sam said, examining the sled. "My grandfather showed me." For the runners, it seems, you take two long rolls of sealskin. You soak them in water, turn up the ends, and let them freeze.

Then you fit some bones for the crossbars and pad them with wet moss. When that is frozen, your sled is ready. He told me that his grandfather once made a sled from the carcass of a musk-ox he had killed, which is one way to bring dinner home.

Tomorrow the two teams separate. Mr. Hobson will go to Cape Felix and search the west coast of King William Land for the place called Ootloolik and the stranded ship. We will continue our march to the south as far as the Great Fish River, then turn back and strike across King William Land to pick up Mr. Hobson's trail. The crews of the *Erebus* and *Terror* must have gone over this ground; there is no other way. But what, now, can we hope to find?

April 28

A brief "Good-bye and good luck," and they were gone in the fog, heading west over the pack. We won't see them again for more than a month, and when we do, what will they have to tell? What will we?

The Captain shot a brace of willow grouse and might have got more if the dogs had not decided to go hunting too. The gunshot didn't alarm the birds—probably they took it for a percussion in the ice, the sound is much the same—but when the dogs started yowling after them, they fluttered out of range. Fresh meat, even if rather raw and feathery, is a welcome change from dry biscuit and the inevitable pemmican.

April 30

Very hard going for the past few days. Deep snow and rough ice underfoot. Sleet driving horizontally. Ice coating everything.

May 1

At home today they will be crowning the May Queen with hawthorn flowers. It's been a long time.

May 3

The weather cleared, and we stayed in camp, chipping ice off the sleds and beating it out of the sleeping bags. We are close to the Magnetic Pole and the Captain spent all day making observations. Using your eyes for close work in this glare is asking for trouble, but I suppose he knows what he is doing.

May 4
MATTY ISLAND

It would be safer to put a query after it: Matty Island? When everything is fractured ice and blown snow, the only way to tell land from sea is to bore for a sounding. Which we haven't done.

A few miles north of here, we came through another Eskimo village. Sled marks, recent ones, pointed away to the west. In all the huts there were wood chips and shavings. Mahogany, oak, ash. The wood must have come from the beached ship, but there was no one left in the village to give us directions to Ootloolik.

We are marching at night now, because of the glare. The Captain admitted ruefully that the only result of his magnetic observations was a case of snow blindness. "The only *immediate* result," he said.

May 6

Rob cannot pull. His legs are too stiff and painful. The Captain put him in charge of the puppy team, the "little miseries," Alec calls them. A month ago that sled would have been the last place for a sick man to rest, but the Captain has done wonders with his ill-matched bunch, and they now work almost as well as the older dogs. They still flop down in the snow, grinning, if the sled is stopped by a hummock or founders in a drift, but even the experienced team does that sometimes.

May 7

I don't think that the people of this village ever saw white men before—alive, that is. They crowded around us, pointing and staring, feeling the cloth of our jackets and the leather of our boots, poking into everything. I felt like some exotic beast in a menagerie. They kept tapping our chests and repeating *"Kammik toome,"* a phrase I hadn't heard before. Their dialect is unfamiliar to both Sam and Mr. Petersen, but eventually they figured it out: *"Kammik toome"* means, "We are friends."

"Kammik toome. Kammik toome." But then I saw one of them pull out a knife and point it at the Cap-

tain. No one else noticed what was happening. As quickly as I could, I got one of the rifles from the sled and leveled it at the man, ready to fire if he made another move. He dropped the knife at once—they know about firearms, evidently—and produced our small saw from behind his back. What I had thought was an attack was just a vigorous attempt to make an exchange, his knife for our saw.

After that, the Captain started bartering in earnest, exchanging needles and knives for anything they had that might have come from the ships. There were bows and arrows of English wood, uniform buttons, silver spoons and forks. I rubbed the handle of one of the forks with my thumb. The grime and tarnish came off quite easily and I saw the monogram: *J. F.* John Franklin?

Mr. Petersen was talking to an old woman, frowning because he was finding it hard to understand her. Suddenly she abandoned words and began to act out her meaning. She shuffled a few steps, leaning forward as if she were pulling a heavy weight behind her. Then she buckled at the knees and fell face down in the snow. It was terribly clear: the men fell down and died as they marched. The men from the lost ships? Who else could it possibly be?

May 12

I promised myself that I wouldn't complain, and so far I've been able to keep the promise. But today has been appalling, the worst day I have ever been through in my whole life. So I'm going to complain—here, now, to myself—for the first and last time.

I am cold . . . cold . . . cold. Even my brain is numb: it is impossible to put two thoughts together. My feet and hands hurt horribly, and my legs are swollen. My ears are sore, and my lips are cracked so badly that I can't drink. I have to suck the tea off the rim of the mug. Most of it spills down my front. Another thing: I can't face the morning. It's cold in the tent, but it's far worse outside. I don't want to go on, not one step further. But in the morning I know that I'll crawl out of my sleeping bag and scrape the ice off my boots and go out into the blizzard again. Why? I don't know why. Because I'm still alive, I suppose.

I thought today that if James were here I would say to him, "Look, James, we're not stubborn, self-righteous Englishmen. We've learned all we can from the Eskimos. We're traveling light, using dogs to help us. We're living off the land, when we can. Our clothes are not much different from theirs—better, perhaps, in some ways. We know what to do about frostbite and snow blindness. *And it is still intolerable.*" But I know what he would answer. He would say, "Think how much worse it would have been if you hadn't learned."

May 17

THE GREAT FISH RIVER

I don't know what I thought, and dreaded, that we would find here. Bones, maybe, and whatever bones can tell. But there is nothing here, nothing at all. We dug in every likely seeming place on the shore and on the island in the frozen estuary and found only an Eskimo cache of blubber marked by two large stones. We took some of it to eke out our kerosene.

May 19

A short march, the first of the journey back. We camped early, hoping that rest would ease the pain in Rob's legs.

May 20

KING WILLIAM LAND

This must be among the worst places in the world.

May 21

We found the skeleton just after midnight. It was lying on the gravel ridge that runs parallel with the shore, face down. The old woman was right: they fell and died as they walked along.

The bones were clean and white. Pieces of cloth lay with them—blue serge, braid, the heavy pilot cloth of a Navy greatcoat. His neckerchief was still tied in a loose bowknot, the kind of knot ship's stewards always use. A clothes brush and a horn comb were next to the thigh-bones, where his pockets would have been. There was a notebook, frozen hard. Perhaps when this is thawed out and we can separate the pages, we'll know who he was.

The only other skeleton I ever saw was the one they kept in the seniors' room at school. Those bones were neatly joined together with wires and screws, the jaws were hinged so that you could look down the throat, and a brass handle protruded from the top of the skull. I never felt that it had been a living man. This was different. There was despair in the way the bones were lying in the snow, with one knee drawn up and the arms flung out to the side. He'd walked and walked until all his strength was gone, dropping farther and farther behind, and no one had seen him fall. Perhaps he had tried to pull himself to his feet and catch up with the others. Or perhaps he had been glad in a way that it was all over. But he had died alone.

We buried him in a shallow stony grave and for a quick moment bared our heads to the bitter wind.

May 23

In this flat, bare land, the hillock at Cape Herschel stands out like a Himalaya. It is about five miles away now, and we can clearly see the cairn on its summit. "Built by one of the Hudson Bay men, mad Thomas Simpson. He came in from the west and this was his farthest point," said Rob. "When? Oh, about twenty years ago, I suppose." Rob seems to have a list of the names, dates, and achievements of Arctic explorers tacked up in the back of his head.

Franklin's men must have gone over this same ground, though they were making their slow way south while we are heading in the opposite direction. If they left any record of their journey anywhere, they would have left it in that cairn on the hill, surely. The Captain thinks so, at any rate, and has ordered an early start tomorrow.

May 24

CAPE HERSCHEL

One side of the cairn had been pulled down, and the stones from the middle dragged out. Someone had been there, looking for whatever might have been buried underneath. We fetched the crowbar and the pickax all the same and dug out the center of the cairn. There were a few loose rocks and below them a huge slab of limestone. We pried it up and heaved it out of the way. There was another slab underneath, and below that—frozen earth. In a fury of disappointment we hacked away until we'd made a hole a good two feet deep. But of course there was nothing there. Whoever had been searching had found what he was looking for. If he was an Eskimo, and if they were books and papers that he found, we'll never get them now. They'll be at the bottom of the sea somewhere.

May 25

Twelve miles north of Cape Herschel we came on a small cairn, newly built just clear of the sea ice. Under a rock at its center was a black metal cylinder. Alec, who found it, handed it to the Captain. There were two pieces of paper inside, rolled up around one another. We watched anxiously as he read, but his face was expressionless and told us nothing at all. Was this good news or bad? At last he looked up and said, "A letter from Mr. Hobson. The cairn marks the farthest point of his march. He is now on his way back to the *Fox*. All his men are well. They have not seen the wreck—the visibility has been poor, with much fog and snow—but at Point Victory, to the north of King William Land, they found . . . they found what so many have sought for so long. It was a printed Navy form, yellowed with age and missing a corner. At the top were blank spaces for the name and position of the ship; below that, a notice printed in six languages: 'Whoever finds this paper is requested to send it to the Admiralty, London, with a note of the time and place at which it was found.' " "A bottle paper," said Rob. "Discovery ships carry them. It's a way of finding out how the currents set."

The Captain went on. There were three messages written on the form. The first read:

> 28 of May 1847. H.M. ships *Erebus* and *Terror* wintered in the ice in lat. 70° 05′ North: long. 92° 23′ West.
> Having wintered in 1845–6 at Beechey Island after having ascended Wellington Channel to lat. 77 and returned by the west side of Cornwallis Island.
> Sir John Franklin commanding the expedition.
> All well.
>
> G. Gore, Lieut.
> Chas. F. Les Voeux, mate.

The second entry was in a different hand, very small and hard to read. It was written along the margins of the paper:

> 25 April 1848. H.M. ships *Terror* and *Erebus* were deserted on the 22 April, 5 leagues N.N.W.

> of this, having been beset since 12 September, 1846. The officers and crews, consisting of 105 souls, under the command of Captain F. R. M. Crozier. Sir John Franklin died on the 11 June, 1847; and the total loss by deaths in the expedition has been to this date 9 officers and 15 men.
>
> James Fitzjames,
> Captain, H.M.S. *Erebus.*

In the last available space was another signature, F.R.M. Crozier, and the final message:

> And start tomorrow, 26, for Back's Great Fish River.

The Captain's voice was shaking.

It was very quiet in the tent. Everyone was thinking about that piece of yellowed paper and the three messages. After supper, the Captain took out a small-scale map. It covered the whole of the Eastern Arctic from Lancaster Sound to Winter Harbor. "Wellington Channel to latitude 77 north," he said, and wrote some figures in the margin. "Back by the *west* of Cornwallis Island. Then south from Beechey Island to latitude 70. That would be Cape Felix or thereabouts." He totaled the figures. "More than five hundred miles in two seasons. And most of it in unknown waters. An extraordinary achievement. I don't know another to equal it." I don't think he realized that he had been talking aloud. He looked surprised when Rob said,

"No, sir, no one's come near it at all, that I've heard." "I think you are right." He looked at the chart again. "Only seventy-odd miles from the point where they were beset to Cape Herschel. And then the map would be finished, from ocean to ocean, and the Northwest Passage would be complete. How impatiently they must have waited for the ice to break up!" "He wrote 'All well,' but after that everthing went wrong," Alec pointed out. "Sir John died. The ice never did break up. Where they planned to sail, they had to go on foot." "They completed the Northwest Passage. They *marched* it," said Rob. "Yes. A chain with one link missing. They put that last link in place—but at what a fearful cost." The Captain's eyes were very sad.

Did the officers know, when they wrote those messages on the Navy form, how little hope there was? Did the men guess? They must have been weak even before they left the ships—24 of them were already dead—and ahead of them was the terrible coast of King William Land and the endless miles of the Great Fish River. I'm sure they knew, every one of those 105 men. They went into it with their eyes open, knowing how small their chances were, but determined to make the attempt rather than die without effort on board the ships. It was a last bold struggle for life.

May 29

LATITUDE 69° 08′ NORTH

The extreme western point of King William Land. The Captain named it Cape Crozier, "To honor the gallant leader of that forlorn hope," he said. Ice coming down from the north is massed twenty feet high on the shore. The wind is so strong that you could lean your weight on it and not fall. I hope, if anyone ever names some piece of land for me, which is unlikely, that it will not be as bleak a place as this.

Rob is worse again. He rode most of the day on the sled, sitting uncomfortably with boxes and bundles around him. There are not nearly as many boxes as there used to be, though. The provisions are getting low, and suppers are smaller. It will be days before we reach the depot.

May 30

From Cape Crozier, the shoreline tends sharply eastward. A few miles along the beach, we came on a boat lying askew across a huge wooden sled. A capital *E,* painted in red on an empty tin can, told us where she had come from. *Erebus.*

She was thirty feet long, painted yellow. An ordinary ship's boat. At least, that's what I thought at first.

Then I saw that all kinds of changes had been made. The stem had been shaved down and the heavy upper strakes had been replaced by thin fir planks. The rudder and its fittings had been taken off and the oars had been cut down to paddles. There had been a canvas rain awning, too, and a sail, though they were in tatters now. She had been equipped for freshwater work. They'd planned to take her across the ice on that monster of a sled and use her for the ascent of the Great Fish River. But in spite of all the alterations she was still terribly heavy. The Captain thought that the boat and the sled together must weigh about 1,800 pounds, "a considerable load for seven strong men in top condition." He didn't have to spell out the rest of it: by the time they started with that load they must have been weak from lack of food.

Snow had filled the boat almost to the gunwales. Digging through it at the bow, we found a pile of clothes, thrown in haphazardly. Coats and jackets, hats, gloves, socks, most of them in rags. There were boots as well—a pair of shooting boots, knee boots with studded soles, sea boots, and a single slipper worked by hand in a checkerboard pattern of red and blue. There were books too: *The Vicar of Wakefield,* two prayer books, a small Bible. But no journals or notebooks, nothing with a name on it. There was a shoemaker's box with all the tools, rolls of sheet lead, three axes, a broken saw, nails, twine, knives, files, sledge irons, leather cartridge cases, a wolfskin robe. I could go on and on. Most of the things were heavy or bulky or awkward to carry. Very few of them were useful. It was an accumulation of dead weight.

They had brought all these things from the ships when they deserted them. They had dragged them over I don't know how many miles of ice and rock, unwilling to part with them for one reason or another. The slipper had been made by his wife, perhaps; the robe was especially warm; the shoemaker's tools might come in handy; the books had always been part of their lives. But here, on this strip of shingle beach, they realized at last just how desperate their situation was.

Gradually we worked our way back to the stern of the boat, shoveling out the snow, turning over the clothes and tools in hopes of finding something that would tell us more about the men who had left them here. We found it by the stern thwart: a corpse, wrapped in furs, lying on the bottom boards. He must have been alive when the others left. Some chocolate and a plug of tobacco had been placed where he could reach them.

"They meant to come back for him, poor fellow." Alec's face was furrowed with pity. "They wouldn't leave a shipmate alone like that. Something must have happened. They must have been cut off, or something. . . ." "No," I said. "I think he knew that they would never come back." "Why d'you say that? That's a dreadful thing to say." "I think he knew that he was dying," I answered slowly. The knowledge of what must have happened had come to me whole in a quick flash of understanding. I had to sort it out. "He knew he didn't have a chance. But the others did. They were almost at the limit of their strength, but they still had a chance. If they took him with them, they'd have to carry him or

drag him on a sled. They'd never get through alive. So he told them to go on without him." "That makes *him* a hero," said Alec. "But what does it make *them?* It makes them selfish brutes." "No, it doesn't. It makes them realists. Leaving him here must have been terribly hard, perhaps the hardest thing they ever did. They cared about him, you can tell. They tried to make him comfortable." "If they cared so much, they would have stayed here with him," Alec replied, unconvinced. "And died," I said. "That's what you're saying–they should have stayed here and died. All of them. But that's wrong, Alec. Look, he was dying. He knew it. They knew it. They had to face reality, however hard it was. They had to weigh the chances for all of them. They decided to go on without him, and I think that they were right."

June 7

Still more than two hundred miles from the *Fox,* and the summer thaw is beginning. The rocks on the southern slopes are bare and wet and there is water running fast under the snow in the ravines. We'll be lucky if we get back before it bursts out and floods the ice.

June 9

We're slogging on, knee-deep in frozen slush, with all the speed we can find. The ice is beginning to give way. Sam said. "This is very bad." On days far worse than this, he never said a word, just kept going, grimly silent. Are the cold and the wind and the endlessness of it all beginning to tell on him?

It must have been weeks since I looked at anyone—really looked, I mean. I'd become used to recognizing them by their outlines. A square, bulky shape was Rob; a short, round one was Sam; the biggest was Mr. Petersen. It was a shock to see how much they have changed. The Captain looks years older. He has a beard now, of course, and there's a lot of gray in it, but it's not only that. His face is pinched and the movements of his arms and hands are stiff. Alec is blotched all over with frostbite, much worse than anyone else. Sam's cheeks used to be so round that they almost hid his eyes; now they are yellow and shrunken. Rob walks like an old man, when he can walk at all. Mr. Petersen has lost pounds in weight; the tendons in his neck are two raveled ropes, mooring his head to his collarbones.

We have been out for sixty-nine days.

June 17

We got the tents up just before the rain started. Rain! There is something very friendly in the way it slaps at the roof of the tent, even in the drip that has started right over my head.

June 19

Back by Long Lake, but all that fast smooth ice is two feet under water now. The dogs have been whipped every step of the way. Their feet are sore, and they hate the rain. There's no way of telling them that it's not much farther.

June 20

The dogs refused to budge, so we left them by Long Lake, huddled under the sleds. The last few miles were easy. We were back on board by noon.

June 22

Mr. Hobson's team got back six days before we did. They had to carry him on to the ship. He couldn't even stand alone. Mr. Young's team is still out. They were forced back to the ship by bad weather a month ago, but left again after a few days. Cooky told me that the doctor protested against their going and would have locked them all up in the hospital cabin if he could.

Raydon died while we were away. " 'E got lower and lower in 'is spirits until 'e wouldn't eat at all," said Cooky. "I made 'im little trays, all fancied up. The only thing missin' was a flower. 'E wouldn't even look at them. We used to take 'im up on deck, the Doctor and me, for fresh air. One day we went to bring 'im below again, and 'e was dead. Just like that." He pinched his fingers together, snuffing out a candlewick. Looking back, I think Raydon was ill even before he got scurvy. He was used up, right from the beginning. It would be hypocrisy to say that I will miss him much, but I'll never forget the night he played the flute for us. Perhaps he meant Lord Randal's refrain for himself: "Make my bed soon, for I'm sick to my heart, and I fain would lie down." They buried him beside Mr. Brands, high up on the beach.

June 23

The Captain asked for volunteers for a search party to look for Mr. Young's men. This time he accepted my offer.

Our dogs were still at Long Lake, curled up asleep, much as we had left them. They had managed to open a tin of pemmican and had eaten that, and their harnesses, of course, and some blubber that we hadn't used. We gave them a good feed, their first in seven days, but they didn't seem unusually hungry and soon went back to sleep.

June 26

The gulley we climbed a week ago on the way up to the lake is a roaring waterfall now. We got back just in time. And there is still no sign of Mr. Young.

June 28

As we rounded the headland at the western end of the strait, we saw them coming along the shore. Creeping, really, and even at that slow pace Old Harvey could barely keep up with the others. Mr. Young was strapped to the dog-sled. They were all terribly thin.

That was yesterday. Tonight everyone is back on board, and Cooky is as happy as a sandboy. The whole crew together again and half-starved at that! Anton had shot a reindeer, so supper was a feast: venison and dried apples and cranberries, followed by pickled whaleskin, for those who could stomach it.

The frostbite scars on my hands are less painful now, so I carved eighty-eight more notches and brought the record up to date.

July 2

Great flocks of ducks and geese have been going over all day. At times their calls almost drowned the noise of Jackson's hammer and the crash of stone ballast dropping into the hold. All the lumber and spare bits and pieces that were put out on the shore last fall have been brought on board, and we are restowing.

July 16

There is open water in the strait now, and the pack is starting to rot in the sun. In the last week, Sam, using Mr. Hobson's rifle, has shot eight seals. He crawls out behind them as they lie basking on the ice, hiding himself behind a little white calico screen. It reminds me of Old Harvey's story about the bears, and I can't help laughing. All I've caught is a trout, and I didn't really catch that. I found a gull and a fox fighting over it and drove them both off.

I've had little time for hunting though. When we'd scrubbed the *Fox* inside and out and she still looked dingy, Mr. Hobson gave out paint, varnish and scrapers and ordered the tar barrel filled. If we weren't all alone, and stuck in this endless ice, you could swear that this was some smart boat club at the start of the yachting season.

July 20

The two graves by the cliff have been sodded over and planted with a little wild lilac-colored flower rather like a snapdragon. I don't know whose work it was. The only other sign of all the months we spent here is a cairn at the entrance to the strait.

August 1

There is open water, but not where we are. The ice is broken up, but the wind keeps it from moving out. It begins to look as though we might be here for another winter. Could we survive it? The lemon-juice ration has been cut in half. Is this because we don't need so much now or because it has to be saved for another season?

August 4

The Captain and the Smith brothers have been fiddling with the engines for days, the manual propped up on a convenient lever. (Mr. Brands wouldn't recognize his book now; all those neat little diagrams are scrawled over with penciled notations and there are greasy fingermarks on every page.) Today they tried their hand at getting up steam, and the boiler primed so violently that water shot up over the topgallant yard.

August 10

The wind has come round at last, and the ice is moving out before it like dust before a new broom.

August 21

At sea—under sail—no land in sight. The pack is behind us, and the rocks and delays and despairs of Prince Regent's Inlet. If I were at the wheel now, the *Fox* would be sailing huge circles, stretching herself in that incredible open space.

August 25

Dead calm. If it weren't for the icebergs, which seem to move with a current too deep to affect us, we might wait it out. As it is, the Captain has gone down to the boiler room, manual in hand, to help "get the steam ready," he he puts it.

A couple of days ago, Sam shot a bear that foolishly swam out to us with her half-grown cub. He asked for some of the meat to give to his mother. I hadn't realized until then that home is only a hundred miles away for him.

August 27

GODHAVN, DISCO ISLAND

Coming into an unmarked harbor on a dark night is a nerve-racking business. You see rocks in the trough of every wave. We steamed in very slowly and dropped anchor safely at three in the morning. A boat was lowered almost before the anchor chain had run out, and Mr. Petersen went ashore for our letters. We could hear him shouting and banging on doors. Then lights showed, dogs started barking, and men ran down to the harbor, dressing as they ran.

There were only a few letters and three or four newspapers, and they were all for the officers. I told myself that I hadn't really been expecting a letter, but I'm no good at fooling myself. Then Mr. Petersen explained that the ice had been so heavy the past spring that none of the whalers, which usually carry the mails from England, had been able to get near the harbor. "So your letters are sailing north," he said cheerfully.

Of course he's cheerful. He is to go on to London with us, and will have to say goodbye almost before he has finished saying hello, but at least he has seen his family and his friends and knows the news. I haven't had a word from home in two years.

Sam packed up and left, taking the haunch of the bear to give to his mother. He didn't say good-bye.

August 28

In spite of my black mood, I went to the dance in the village hall. It was a great success, and we're staging another tonight, to return hospitality.

Rob played the accordion and there was a fiddler from the village. He knew none of Rob's tunes and Rob knew none of his, but it didn't matter; they grinned at the discords. We knew none of the Eskimos' dance steps and they knew none of ours, but that didn't matter either. We hopped or jumped or tried scraps of jigs or polkas or simply stamped in time with whichever instrument had the better tune. The dance went on for hours, getting wilder and noisier and faster and giddier, until we were too weary to pick our feet up off the floor.

In the middle of the evening, Sam came into the hall, with an old woman on one side and a young one on the other. He pulled them after him through the crowd and introduced me. The older one was his mother, as I had guessed. The other was his sister, Marie. It is strange that he never mentioned her. She was the belle of the evening, and not only because she was wearing white gloves and a scented handkerchief with the usual fur trousers. She danced like a feather, like a little brown bird, like an india-rubber ball.

August 30

Two nights of dancing have undone me. I woke late and spent an hour over breakfast as if I had nothing to do all day. And, in fact, the Eskimos have taken over most of our usual harbor chores. A gang of girls has scrubbed the deck and the paintwork. The men have brought in fresh water and stone ballast and sand. We have had time to loll in the sun with back numbers of the Copenhagen illustrated papers.

Sam and Anton were discharged today. I asked Sam what he was going to do with his pay. "Get a rifle," he said, without a second's hesitation. "Much better than a harpoon." "Anything else? You'll have money left over." "I buy wood, build a house, marry a nice girl, and be a rich old lazy man." I laughed with him, but I was sad too. The time he spent with us has changed him. He's not content with the old ways any longer. But if I were in his place, I'd probably feel the same.

He reached inside his shirt and handed me something. It was wrapped in transparent seal gut—he's still very much an Eskimo. "Open it," he urged. "I make it for you." Inside was an oblong piece of soapstone, so smooth that it looked as if it had been waxed. There was a hole at one end, with a fine thong through it. He slipped it over my head. "It is good luck," he said, and was gone before I could find words to thank him.

After that, I went to say good-bye to the dogs. They were out on the rocks, at the point nearest to the ship. They still seem to feel that the *Fox* is where they belong, though they all have new masters now. A couple of them twitched their ears when I patted them; the rest didn't stir. Lazy beasts! But they never flinched or missed a step in all the days that our lives depended on them, and they've earned their sleep in the sun.

The good-luck stone is cool on my skin. I feel wretched that I didn't make something to give him. But what? Almost anything I can do, he does far better.

September 10

Greenland is behind us now, and the last of the icebergs. The air seems warmer already. They are singing as they pull in the slack.

> Rolling home, rolling home,
> Rolling home across the sea.
> Rolling home to Merry England,
> Where kind friends do wait for me.

September 11

I went aloft with Alec and Rob to bend a new topsail. The old one was worn to streamers. When we'd done, I looked down and thought, It's now or never. Then I spat on my hands and slid down the backstay. My stom-

ach stayed up there in the yards somewhere, but it was a glorious feeling all the same. "Well, well!" said Rob, when he had picked his way down the shrouds. "I always thought that we would make a sailor of you."

September 14

About four hundred miles from Land's End. We've made a quick passage. The last few days have been very rough, with huge seas boiling up over the stern and sluicing across the deck. After two years in the still Arctic waters, I'd forgotten what it was like to be in a sea like this. I think everyone had—and everyone is feeling it.

September 17

A light way over to port. Flash-flick-flash . . . flash-flick-flash. Portland Bill? St. Alban's Head? That's Mr. Hobson's worry; he's the navigator. All that matters to me is that it's an English light.

September 20

Sails all around and more on the horizon. I saw a brigantine, a pair of matched schooners racing down the channel to Cowes, fishing boats, a big three-masted merchantman. Then what I'd been waiting for: the red-mud canvas and the jaunty gaff of a Lowestoft wherry.

The land is only a flat brown line between sea and sky, but the air smells of leaves and smoke. Not long now.

September 21

LONDON

We came up the Thames under our own steam. Past the sand flats at Canvy Island. Past dusty late-summer trees and fields of hops and ripening wheat and green, green grass. Past Gravesend and the docks and boys fishing off the ferry slip. Past West Ham and Greenwich. Past barges and tall, top-heavy warehouses and the smell of coffee and lumber and fish. Up to the Pool of London. "Half speed, both engines." "Dead slow." "Reverse her now . . . easy . . . easy." And we slid alongside the wharf without a bump.

September 26

My last night on the *Fox*. Everything is packed. The ship is very bare, all her gear ashore. Only the iron-shod prow and the long scratches above the waterline show where she's been. Apart from those, she might be any small steam yacht, brought up to London for a refit.

Cooky and Dusty and Jackson have gone home already, though they'll be back tomorrow for the presentation. Alec has a long journey ahead of him before he sees his Betty. He's leaving the Navy now for good. Rob says that he'll look for another berth. "The China Seas perhaps, for a change." But I think that the north will pull him back—it's not everyone who was born on a whaler. As for me, I'll travel home in style. There's more money in my pockets than I've ever seen before. I could easily have spared five guineas toward the gift we're getting for the Captain, but Old Harvey only asked for a half sovereign and wouldn't take more.

It's all over now bar the shouting, and the newspapers have done that for us. We've been on the front pages for five days, and still to come is a long article in *The Illustrated London News*, complete with drawings and "the impressions of John Micklethwaite, the youngest hand on board the *Fox*, exclusive to this paper." They will probably make nonsense of what I said. Most of the things that have been written about the voyage and what we accomplished have been well wide of the mark. We aren't a "little band of heroes"—

just look at us. What we did wasn't a "selfless endeavor." More important, to call Franklin's expedition "ill-fated" and leave it at that is to tell only half the story. They had more than their share of bad luck, but they also had more than their share of courage. Don't the people who write for the newspapers have any idea what it must have been like to be beset for nineteen months—to watch sickness creep into the ships—to bury your captain and your shipmates—and then to complete the Northwest Passage on foot and die alone in the snow with no one to close your eyes?

September 27

Mr. Hobson and Old Harvey chose a gold chronometer for the Captain and had it engraved, *With deep respect from the officers and crew of the* Fox. *1857–1859.* Alec said, "They should have put in 'gratitude,' or something like that. I mean it. After all, he got us back alive." But I agree with Old Harvey: "deep respect" says what we mean to say about him as a man and as a captain.

We assembled on deck at noon, for the last time. I found myself looking for the faces I knew I wouldn't see: James, Dick Singleton, Mr. Brands, Raydon. And Anton and Sam.

Old Harvey, ram-rod straight in a new jacket and all

his medals, presented the chronometer in its mahogany box. I was expecting him to make a speech—he'd been muttering over a piece of paper since breakfast—but all he said was, "This is for you, sir, from all . . . from all of us, that is." I think Captain McClintock was genuinely surprised. He took the chronometer out of its box, turned it over, and read the inscription. He said very simply, "How can I thank you all? I am more touched by this than I can say."

Then it was good-bye. I was the last to leave, except the Captain. When I went down the gangway, he was standing by the wheel, the box under his arm, looking up at the northern sky.

The officers and ship's company of the FOX.

F. L. McClintock . . . . Captain, R.N.

W. R. Hobson . . . . Lieutenant, R.N.

Allen W. Young . . . . Captain, Mercantile Marine. Sailing master.

David Walker, M.D. . . . . Surgeon.

George Brands . . . . Engineer

Carl Petersen . . . . Interpreter.

James Pride* . . . . Second Engineer.

Harvey Lloyd* . . . . Chief Quartermaster.

Robert Harmsworth* . . . . Captain of Hold.

Alexander Macrae* . . . . Sailmaker.

Richard Jackson* . . . . Carpenter.

David Thomas* . . . . Carpenter's mate.

Raydon Jones* . . . . Boatswain's mate.

Charles (Cooky) Andrews* . . . . Steward.

Steve Smith* . . . . Stoker.

Sy Smith* . . . . Stoker.

Richard Singleton* . . . . A.B

Dusty Miller* . . . . A.B.

John Micklethwaite* . . . . A.B.

Michael McDaniel* . . . . Officers' steward.

Samuel Emanuel . . . . Dog driver.

Anton Christian . . . . Dog driver.

Four other crewmen, not named.

**fictional name.*

GLOSSARY

AFT—in or near stern of ship.

BACKSTAY—rope slanting abaft from the masthead to a lower point.

BEAM—the side of a ship.

BEAT—to sail against the wind, to tack.

BOLT-ROPE—a rope sewn all around the edge of a sail, to prevent it from tearing.

BOOM—long spar with one end attached, stretching foot of sail.

BOW—fore-end of a boat or ship.

COMPANIONWAY—staircase to cabin.

CROW'S NEST—shelter for lookout man at masthead, often a barrel.

DECLINOMETER—instrument for measuring magnetic declination.

FO'C'SLE (FORECASTLE)—forward part under deck where sailors live.

FOOTROPE—a rope extended beneath a yard on which sailors stand when furling or reefing the sail.

FORE—situated in front.

FOREMAST—forward lower mast of ship.

GALLEY—ship's kitchen.

GANGWAY—opening in bulwarks by which ship is entered or left; bridge laid across from this to shore.

HALYARD—rope, tackle, for raising or lowering sail, yard, etc.

HATCHWAY—trapdoor over an aperture in the deck.

HEAD (MASTHEAD)—top of mast.

HOLD—cavity in ship below deck, where cargo is stowed.

HOVE-TO—brought to a standstill without anchoring or making fast.

LEE—the sheltered side, the side away from the wind.

LOG—float attached to line wound on reel for gauging speed of ship.

MAINMAST—principal mast.

MAINSAIL—sail set on after part of mainmast.

MIZZENMAST—aftermost mast of a three-masted ship.

PORT—left-hand side of a ship, looking forward.

RATLINES—small lines fastened across shrouds like ladder-rungs.

REEF—one of three or four strips across top of a square sail and bottom of a fore-and-aft sail, that can be taken in to reduce the sail's surface. Reef, verb—to take in reefs.

RIGGING—the ropes or chains used to support the masts (standing rigging) and to work or set the yards, sails, etc. (running rigging or running gear).

RUDDER—broad flat wooden or metal piece hinged to vessel's sternpost for steering with.

RUN—to sail straight and fast.

RUNNING GEAR—see Rigging.

SHORTEN SAIL—to reduce the amount of sail spread.

SHROUDS—set of ropes leading from the head of the mast; part of the standing rigging.

SPAR—stout pole used for mast, yard, etc. of ship.

STANDING RIGGING—see Rigging.

STARBOARD—right-hand side of a ship, looking forward.

STEM—curved timber or metal piece to which ship's sides are joined at fore end.

STERN—hind part of a ship or boat.

STERN SHEETS—place in boat aft of rowers' thwarts, often with seats for passengers.

STRAKE—continuous line of planking from stem to stern of ship.

THEODOLITE—surveying instrument for measuring vertical and horizontal angles by means of a telescope.

THWART—oarsman's bench placed across boat.

TOPGALLANT—topgallant sail or yard, those immediately above topmast or topsail.

TOPMAST—next above lower mast.

TOPSAIL—square sail next above lowest.

WATCH—four-hour spell of duty on board ship; one of the halves into which ship's crew is divided to take alternate duty.

WEATHER—windward.

YARD—a spar slung at its center from, and forward of, a mast and serving to support and extend a square sail.